THE DWARFS

Harold Pinter was born in 1930. His plays include: *The Birthday Party, The Caretaker, The Homecoming, Old Times, No Man's Land* and *Betrayal.* Screenplays include: *The Servant, Accident, The Go-Between, The French Lieutenant's Woman, A La Recherche Du Temps Perdu, The Heat of the Day, The Comfort of Strangers.*

The Dwarfs

A Novel

HAROLD PINTER

———

faber and faber
LONDON · BOSTON

First published in 1990
by Faber and Faber Limited
3 Queen Square London WC1N 3AU
This paperback edition first published in 1992

Printed in England by Clays Ltd, St Ives plc

A CIP record for this book is available from the British Library

ISBN 0-571-16417-X

To Judy Daish

AUTHOR'S NOTE

I wrote *The Dwarfs* in the early fifties, before I began writing plays. I didn't offer it for publication at the time.

In 1960 I extracted some elements from the book and wrote a short play under the same title. The play is quite abstract, mainly, I believe, because I omitted the essential character of Virginia from it.

In 1989 I read the book for the first time in many years and decided it would benefit from further work. This work consisted mainly of cuts. I cut five chapters which seemed to me redundant and reorganized or condensed a number of other passages. Despite this reshaping, the text is fundamentally that written over the period 1952–1956.

I

One

Just before midnight they went to the flat. It was dark and the blinds were down. Len unlocked the front door and pushed it open. A pile of letters lay on the mat. He picked them up and put them on the hall table. They walked down the stairs. Pete opened the living-room window and took a packet of tea from his pocket. He went into the kitchen and filled the kettle.

Len adjusted his glasses and followed. From his inside pocket he drew out a recorder. He blew into it, held it up to the light and put it to his mouth. Bending, he shook it violently and polished it on his trousers, rose, seized a stiff dishcloth from the towelrack and wiped his fingers. He then wiped the recorder, twiddled it between his fingers, put it to his mouth, set his fingers on the holes and blew. There was no sound.

– Don't overdo it.

Len tapped the recorder on his head.

– What's the matter with it? he said.

The rain fell on the kitchen roof. Pete waited for the kettle to boil, poured water into the teapot and took it into the living room, where he set two cups on the table. By the fireplace stood two armchairs, facing. He sat down in one of them and lit a cigarette.

– There's something wrong with this recorder, Len said.

– Let's have some tea.

– I can't do a thing with it.

Len poured the tea and slapped his pockets.

– Where's the milk? he asked.

– You were going to bring it.

– That's right.

– Well, where is it?

– I forgot it. Why didn't you remind me?

- Give me the cup.
- What do we do now?
- Give me the tea.
- Without milk?
- Come on.
- Without any milk?
- There isn't any milk.
- What about sugar? Len asked, passing the cup.
- You were going to bring it.
- Why didn't you remind me?

Pete looked about the room.

- Well, he said, everything looks in good order.
- Hasn't he got any?
- Any what?
- Sugar.
- I couldn't find any.
- It's like the workhouse here.

From a hook by the fireplace Pete lifted a toasting fork with a monkey's head and examined it.

- This is interesting.
- That? Len said. Haven't you ever seen that before? It's Portuguese. Everything in this house is Portuguese.
- Why's that?
- That's where he comes from.
- So he does.
- Or at least, his grandfather on his mother's side.

Pete slipped the fork back on the hook.

- Well, well.
- Or his grandmother on his father's side.

The hall clock chimed. They listened.

- What time is he coming?
- About half-past one.
- Well, what about a shot of air?
- Air? Len said.
- What's the matter with that thing?
- There's nothing wrong with it. It's the best on the market.

4

But it must be broken. It's a year since I played it.

Pete stood up, yawned, and strolled to the bookshelf. The books, closely stacked, were covered in dust. On the bottom shelf he found a Bible. He looked at the inscription.

– I gave him this, years ago, he said.

– What?

– This Bible.

– What for?

Pete pushed the book back and brushed his fingers.

– This tea's murder on the liver, Len said.

– Well, what about it?

– What about what?

– A shot of air.

– Not me.

– Why not?

– It's raining.

– Listen, Pete said.

– I can't hear a thing.

– The rain's stopped.

– How do you know?

– Can you hear it?

– No.

– You can't hear it because it's stopped.

– Anyway, Len said, the rain's got nothing to do with it.

– Have mercy.

– No, I know where you'll drag me.

– Where?

– Over the Lea.

– Well?

– You don't know what it's like there at night.

– Don't I?

– All right, you do know. You may know. But you're prepared to go over there again at night. I'm not.

– Do you know, Pete said, I think it's about time you bucked your ideas up. You're at death's door.

He sat down. Len took out a handkerchief and wiped his

5

glasses, smiling. He then placed his glasses on the table, stood up, sneezed twice and shook his head.

– I've got the most shocking blasted cold I've ever had in all my life.

He blew his nose.

– Still, it's not much of a nuisance, really.

Pete sat looking at the sooted newspaper in the fireplace, tapping his foot on the hearth.

– Here, Len said, shall I go and get my fiddle and play you a few titbits while you're in the mood? I've got a piece of Alban Berg up my sleeve would make you see stars.

– Has he ever written to you in red ink? Pete asked.

– Eh?

– Red ink. There's a bottle on the bookshelf.

– Of course he has. What about it? Has he ever written to you in red ink?

– No.

Len sneezed and blew his nose. The rain began to fall again, beating on the window. Leaning across the table, he pressed his nose to the pane.

– It's dark.

– Take some friar's balsam, Pete said.

– Why? Have you ever written to him in red ink?

Pete took his cup into the kitchen and rinsed it out. He returned to the living room to find Len, eyes screwed, holding his glasses at arm's length before him.

– It's still there.

– What now?

– You don't know what you're missing by not wearing glasses.

– What am I missing? Pete asked, pouring tea into his cup.

– I'll tell you. You see, there's always a point of light in the centre of the lens, in the centre of your sight. You can't go wrong. You can't miss your step. There's always, even in the darkest night, a pinch, a fragment of light, poised in front of you. Look here, there are some people, you know

6

as well as I do, who go around with a continual crease in their forehead. When, at times, they manage to eliminate that crease, the world's right, they'd invest in anything. Well, all right, I'm not saying I have the same outlook, just because there are times I realize this square of light exists. Nowhere near the same outlook. But all I'll say is this. What this point of light does, it indicates the angle of your orbit. There's no need to look at me like that. You don't under-stand. It gives you a sense of direction, even if you never move from the one spot.

– Do I have to go down on my bended knees?
– I'm giving you a hot tip.
– Just answer one question, Pete said. Don't you go around yourself with a continual crease in your forehead?
– Exactly. Precisely. That's why I know what I'm talking about.

The hall clock struck one. Len slipped on his glasses and sat still.

– Ten to one he'll be hungry.
– Why?
– I'll lay odds.

Pete closed his eyes and lay back.

– He can eat like a bullock, that bloke, Len said.

He turned the recorder in his hands.

– I've seen him finish off a loaf of bread before I'd got my jacket off.

He put the recorder to his left eye and looked into it.

– He'd never leave a breadcrumb on a plate in the old days.

Pete opened his eyes, lit a match and watched it burn.

– Of course he may have changed, Len said, standing up and moving about the room. Things do change. But I'm the same. Do you know I had five solid square meals one day last week. At eleven o'clock, two o'clock, six o'clock, ten o'clock and one o'clock. Not bad going. Work makes me hungry. I was working that day.

He leaned against the cupboard and yawned.

7

- I'm always starving when I get up. Daylight has a funny effect on me. As for the night, that goes without saying. As far as I'm concerned the only thing you can do in the night is eat. It keeps me fit, especially if I'm at home. I have to run downstairs to put the kettle on, run upstairs to finish what I'm doing, run downstairs to cut a sandwich or arrange a salad, run upstairs to finish what I'm doing, run back downstairs to see to the sausages, if I'm having sausages, run back upstairs to finish what I'm doing, run back downstairs to lay the table, run back upstairs to finish what I'm doing, run back –
- Yes!
- Where did you get those shoes?
- What?
- Those shoes. How long have you had them?
- Why, what's the matter with them?
- I'm losing my grip. Have you been wearing them all night?
- No, Pete said. I walked from Bethnal Green in my naked feet.
- I must be losing my grip.
He sat at the table and shook his head.
- When did you last sleep? Pete asked.
- Sleep? Don't make me laugh. All I do is sleep.
- What about work? How's work?
- Euston? An oven. It's an oven. Still, bad air is better than no air, I suppose. It's best on nightshift. The trains come in, I give a bloke half a dollar, he does my job, I curl up in a corner and read the timetables. The canteen's always open. If I was there tonight they'd give me a cup of tea with as much milk and sugar as I wanted, I can tell you that.
Pete stood up and stretched, pressing his hand against the wall.
- You could do with a bit more weight, Len said. You're made of bone.
- He'll be here in a minute.
- Have you looked at your cheekbones lately? They're coming through your skin.

8

– What about it? Pete said, peering out of the window.

Len took off his glasses and rubbed his eyes.

– I think I'm undergoing a change, he said.

– Are you?

– I feel it. I feel I'm undergoing a change.

Pete collected the teapot and cups and took them into the kitchen, where he put the kettle on the gas.

– What's going on? asked Len, in the doorway.

– He'll want a beverage.

– Black tea? You're mad. You can't welcome a man back to his own home with a cup of black tea.

– Collect your thoughts, Pete said. What did you tell me he wrote to you in his letter?

– He said go to the flat and put the kettle on.

– For tea?

– For tea.

– That's exactly what I'm doing, Pete said. In fact, I'm interpreting his words in their strictest sense. He's going to get tea. Black tea. Pure tea. At one and nine a quarter.

The bell rang.

– That's the man, Pete said. Open the door.

Two

– Did you sleep?

– I slept all day, Mark said.

– Come in.

Len closed the door. They walked down the stairs into the kitchen.

– What do you think of my kitchen? Has it changed?

Mark took a comb from his pocket and combed his hair.

– It remains a kitchen of the highest possible class, he said.

– Look here, Mark, Len said, I'm glad you had a good sleep. Listen. What do you think of this book? I want you to have a sniff at it. You've never seen anything like it. I can guarantee that.

Mark put his comb in his pocket and looked at the title.

– *Reimman's Theory of Integrals*. What are you trying to do, lead me into temptation?

– Why don't you read it? Len said. It's right up your street.

– Next Tuesday a fortnight, Mark said, you can start me on a course.

– You're missing the opportunity of a lifetime.

– Mathematics, chess and ballet dancing. You've got to start at the age of twelve, eleven.

– You don't know what you're talking about.

– Even before.

– Listen, Len said. All last night I was working at mechanics and determinants. There's nothing like a bit of calculus to cheer you up. Can't you see? It's dead. It can't eat you. The mind jumps over the gate and walks in air.

– No?

– I'm telling you, I tell you. It's the only time I feel that I'm anything like an eachway bet.

– What's this? Mark said, lifting a piece of paper from between the pages.

– What is it?

– It's one of your poems.

Len snatched it, read it quickly and crumpled it into his pocket.

– What's the matter? said Mark. Let me have a look at it.

– It's gibberish, Len said. There's no point. It's leprous.

He took it out of his pocket and stuffed it into the bin under the sink.

– It's out of the question.

– I believe you.

Len frowned, rasped, and did up his shirtsleeves.

– What about Pete? Mark said. Has he been writing anything lately?

– I don't know. How would I know? It's not my business. But he's got other kettles on the boil. That I do know.

– Has he?

– Yes.

– I wonder that they are.

– You're entitled to wonder.

Mark smiled, and looked about him at the bare kitchen. The ceiling was low. The dresser, chairs and table were plain, of a light coloured wood. By the wall, the boiler bulged. It was a square room. A small window looked out on to the yard.

– The rooms, he said, we live in.

– Don't tell me, don't mention it, said Len.

His wrists jerked, gesturing. He shook his head and clicked his teeth.

– The rooms we live in open and shut.

From under the table he grated a chair, began to sit, shoved the chair back and moved to rap the wall.

– They change shape at their own will, he said. I would have no quarrel, I wouldn't grumble, you see, if these rooms would remain the same, would keep to some consistency. But they don't. And I can't see the boundaries, the limits,

11

which I've been led to believe are natural. That's the trouble. I'm all for the natural behaviour of rooms, doors, staircases, the lot. But I can't rely on them. When, for example, I look through a train window, at night, and see the yellow lights, very clearly, I see what they are, and I see that they're still. But they're only still because I'm moving. I know that they do move along with me, and when we go round a bend, they bump off. But I know that they are still, just the same. They are, after all, stuck on poles which are rooted in the earth. So they must be relatively still, in their own right, in so far as the earth itself is still, which of course it isn't, but that's another matter. The point is, in a nutshell, that I can only appreciate such facts when I'm moving. When I'm still, nothing around me follows a natural course of conduct. I'm not saying I'm any criterion myself. I wouldn't say that. After all, when I'm on that train I'm not really moving at all. That's obvious. I'm in the corner seat. I'm still. I am, perhaps, being moved, but I do not move. Neither do the yellow lights. The train moves, granted, but what's a train got to do with it?

- Quite, said Mark.
- So where are you? I'm quite prepared to admit that this isn't an open and shut case. But offhand I can't think of any case that's open and shut. Quite frankly, I can't even think of a case. There isn't, let's face it, a shred of evidence. It wouldn't stand a chance in court. The judge would have a fit and I'd lose my licence.
- No question.
- It's no joke.
- Hardly.
- Does the jury move?
- Eh?
- No. On the bench they're still. And I'm still in the dock. No change. When I move though, in this case, so do they. I go down the hutch and they call a cab.
- That's it.

– Change but no change. But where does all this solve my problem? Can you tell me that? No, of course you can't. It is so, that's all. And it will be so. Perhaps we are not guilty. Are we? Pete would say we are guilty. You would say we are not. Are we?

– No, Mark said. We're not.

Len laughed. He opened the basement door and breathed in. It was raining.

– Well, Mark said, there's only one thing I've got to say.

– What's that?

– When you're in you're in.

– What? Len said. What did you say? When you're in you're in?

– Sure.

– You're right. I can't deny it. You've never said a truer word. When you're in, he repeated, walking round the table, you're in. That's it. You can knock me down with a feather. I must remember that. What made you say a thing like that?

– It just struck me. When you're in you're in.

– Well, said Len, I'll have to grant you that. You can't get away from it. It stands to reason. And when you're not in you're out. Or, more accurately, when you're out you're not in.

– Yes, that's more like it.

– When you're in, Len muttered, you're in, eh? Well, I'll have to store that one up for a hard winter.

Upstairs, in the living room, Mark leaned back in the frayed leather armchair, regarding the circle of light on the ceiling, while Len, carefully lifting his violin from its case and adjusting the bow, concentrated on a passage of Bach, scowling and snapping at the false notes.

– I can't do it, he declared.

There was a thump at the backdoor. He twisted the doorknob. The cat screwed through and scrabbled under the table.

– It's ridiculous. I must practise. My fingers are as sensitive as an ironmangle. I'd do better cleaning windows.

13

– Sounded all right to me, Mark said.

– No, no. It's an insult to Bach. It's an impertinence. The trouble is, he murmured, packing the violin, that when I find some direction for my energies I can't sustain it. I should. I should do nothing but practise my music. Come to a working arrangement and stick to it. But look at it. I've been a farmhand, a builder's mate, a packer, a stagehand, a shipping clerk, I've dug turf, I've been a hop picker, a salesman, a postman, I'm a railway porter, a mathematician, a fiddle-player, I scribble and I play a fair game of cricket. I haven't touched pearldiving and I've never been a male nurse. What sort of set-up's that? It's ludicrous. I've never been able to look into the mirror and say, this is me. What's that cat up to?

The cat was jolting in spasms against the door.

– What's the matter? Len said. All right. Go out. I can quite understand it.

– I'm not sure, Mark said, watching the tail flick into the night, that there's not more to that cat than meets the eye.

Len closed the door.

– Let's go downstairs, he said quietly.

– We've just come up.

– I know. Let's go down.

– Down we go, Mark said.

They walked down the wooden steps into the basement. Len switched on the kitchen light. Mark sat down, yawned and lit a cigarette.

– Ah well.

– Do you know, Len said, I'm never quite sure that you understand one word I'm talking about.

– What?

– You may understand, of course, or it may be that when you open your mouth you take a shot in the dark which might or might not be relevant. If that's it, you're a pretty fair shot, I'll give you that. But I sometimes get the impression that you do nothing but study form. Pete, for instance, will

14

always let me know when he doesn't understand what I'm saying, in one way or another. He feels it's a moral duty. You very rarely do that. What does that mean? Does it mean that you never want to commit yourself? Or does it mean that you've got nothing to commit?

Mark flicked his ash on to the stone floor. It fell without breaking shape. With the point of his shoe he dispersed it gently, grinding it by the tableleg. He looked up at Len.

– Were you saying something?

– Where were you acting? Huddersfield?

– That's right.

– Did they like you in Huddersfield?

– They loved me.

– What's it like when you act? Does it please you? Does it please anyone else?

– What's wrong with acting?

– It's a time-honoured profession. It's time-honoured. It goes without saying. But what does it do? Does it please you when you walk on to a stage and everybody looks up and watches you? Maybe they don't want to watch you at all. Maybe they'd prefer to watch someone else. Have you ever asked them?

Mark laughed and lit a cigarette. Len sat at the table, gritting his teeth, and banged his forehead.

– Do you know what I am? I'm an agent for a foreign power.

The doorbell rang.

Through the coalhole grating, Pete glimpsed a stab of light into the cellar from the inner basement. He leaned at the door's side. A light wind scuttled in the low hedge. The moon blinked between turning clouds. A black cat, wiry, leapt up the steps, trod over his boot and sat close-eyed at the door. Its tail flicked his ankle. He looked down at the hunched shape. The cat pressed its nose to the crack. They waited in silence.

Len opened the door. The cat ducked between his legs into the hall.

- What's that?
- A cat.
- Your cat?
- My cat? said Pete. What are you talking about? I haven't got a cat.
- Haven't you?
- Well, come on, let me in.
- I suppose it must be my cat, Len muttered, closing the door behind them.
- It could only be your cat.
- Why? What makes you say that?
- We had a little chat, Pete said, on your doorstep.
- What about?
- The theory of numbers.
- What did he have to say?
- Don't wear me out, Pete said. I'm not up to it. Why don't you switch on a few lights? This place is like the black hole of Calcutta.

Mark was sitting with his feet up on the table.

- What ho, Pete said.
- Greetings.
- I don't trust that cat, Len said. I let him out the back door and he comes in the front.
- What about a shake in the air? There's a good delousing wind out. Open to all comers. You both look as if you could do with it.

Mark swung his legs to the floor.

- You're right. Let's get out.
- Perhaps you'd like to hear a little serenade before you go, said Len. It's by Spack and Rutz and played by Yetta Clatta. It's church music.
- Another time, Weinblatt, Pete said.

They left the house and walked to the duckpond. On a bench by the wooden bridge they spread a newspaper and sat down. Wind tipped the hanging rain from the leaves.

- Listen here, Pete, Len said. Why do you always call me Weinblatt? My name's Weinstein. Always has been.
- It won't stick.

Mark began to cough, his cough growing to a rolling grate. Swearing between gasps, he staggered to the pond's edge and spat copiously. Clearing his throat, he spat again, into the dark water.

- Mark, Pete said, you're out on your own as a gobber.
- Thanks, Mark said, spitting into a bush.

He sat down and wiped his mouth.

- But what I want to know is, Pete said, when are you going to give up rattling and put on a cowl?
- Me? What do you mean? I am a priest. Nowhere am I so religious as in bed. I put them all in touch with the universe.
- What you mean is you lead them all up the garden.
- Exactly.

Len had risen, and was standing by the pond, his hands in his pockets.

- I've signed my name to something, he said.
- Joined the army? Mark asked.
- No, Len said, sitting down. I've applied for a job in an insurance office.
- Don't say that.
- What do you mean? Pete said. See if he can stick it.
- I know what'll happen, Len said. They'll have me doing mortality tables all day. I'll sit and calculate the next best mortality rate. A bloke like you, Mark, only gets the next best, not the best.
- What about a bloke like me? said Pete.
- Why should you get the best? I don't know anyone who gets the best.
- What about your cat? asked Mark.
- You could stick it, Pete said, with a bit of go and guts.

Pete and Mark lit cigarettes. Len watched their heads bend to the match.

- It's no joke, this job business, Mark said, smoke slipping from his nose.
- Well, Len said, it all depends on which way you look at it. For instance, I know a geezer who's always touching wood. So you know what he did? He took a job in a library. Look at all the chances there are for touching wood in a library. The place is full of wood. He has the time of his life.

Len stood up.

- Look here, Pete, he said. Let's have a look at your hand.
- My hand?
- Yes.

He lifted Pete's left hand to his chin, lowered his glasses and peered at the palm. Breathing through his teeth, he bent closer. With a start he let the hand drop.

- You're a homicidal maniac! he exclaimed. I thought as much.
- What! said Mark.
- Give me that hand, Len demanded. Look, I ask you, at that hand. Look. A straight line right across the middle. Right across the middle. Horizontal. See? That's all he's got. What else has he got? I've never seen anything like it. You're a nut!
- It's very likely, Pete said.
- Very likely? You couldn't find two men in a million with a hand like that. It sticks out a mile. You're a homicidal maniac. Without a shadow of a doubt. We can lay our last bets.

Len was on nightshift. He left them to catch his bus. Pete and Mark began to walk towards Bethnal Green.

- Do you know what he's up to? Pete said.
- No. What?
- He's started to read the New Testament.
- And the very best of luck.
- I came across that Bible I gave you the other day.
- Where?
- On your bookshelf.

18

- Oh yes.
- Have you ever read it?
- Well, to tell you the truth, Pete, I haven't quite got round to it yet.
- You've had it about five years. What do I keep you for?
- No, I need a holiday first, before I can have a go at it.
- It's about time you branched out, Pete said. Do yourself a favour.
- You can never tell.

They turned the corner by the Electricity Company.

- What do you know about love? Pete said.
- Love?
- Yes, you must know something about it.
- What makes you say that?

A sudden shower drove them into the doorway of a bookshop. They watched the rain bounce on the steps of the police station. A policeman came out of the station and looked across the road.

- Well, Mark said, this is the best secondhand bookshop in the East of London, Clive.
- I must say it looks impressive.
- Isn't that the *Yellow Book*, just behind the black book?
- It's something to do with artichokes, Pete said, bending.

The policeman walked across the road towards them.

- Ethiopian architecture I think it was.
- What was?
- That book I nearly bought.
- Oh that one. I thought it was *Logic and Colic* by Blitz.
- Oh no, Mark said, you're thinking of *Dust* by Crutz.
- Am I?

The policeman walked past the doorway.

- Good health.
- Let's go the other way, Mark said.
- Anyway, Pete said, as they stepped into the street, it sticks out a mile you're the right bloke to ask about love.
- Does it? Why?
- The point is this, Pete said. I've got a few ideas for some

love stories for women's magazines.

- What?
- Yes. But I start out with a working deficiency, because I know next to nothing about the subject. But I was thinking, if you could give me a few hot tips, it shouldn't take me long to get the whole business taped.
- You're pulling my whatsit.
- Cross my heart, I'm not. I'm dead serious. It'll do me good to try my hand at the game. Why not? Well, come on. What's it all about?
- Do me a favour.
- What's the matter? You've been up to your knees in this lovelark for years.
- That's right, Mark said. It makes the world go round.
- How does a bloke in love feel? What are his feelings?
- Look, why don't you find out for yourself?
- How do I go about it?

They walked under the railway bridge.

- All right, Mark said. You've brought it up. What's the position between you and Virginia?
- We've got a lot in common.
- But you wouldn't say you loved her?
- That question might even be relevant, Pete said. But I can't answer it.
- Does the blood flow?
- What do you mean?
- Does it flow?
- The blood? Well, I'll tell you. We don't go in for it much these days.
- You don't?

Crowds were leaving the Hackney Empire. They crossed the road.

- No. The way I look at it is this. It was an unknown factor I had to solve and I solved it – years ago – and it's not much use to me now.
- It's not, eh?

– No.
– Well, Mark said, I think you could do yourself a bit of good to give it another run.
– No. I don't think that's the answer to anything.
Crossing by the trafficlights and moving towards Cambridge Heath they smelt soap, crisp and insistent in the street.
– Where is it? Mark sniffed. Where's the factory? Where is it?
– Somewhere over there, Pete pointed.
They looked across the street and, under the sootwalls of an arch, saw the chimneys, wasteland and dark warehouses.
– Of course, it may not exist at all. May be God letting out the bath.
– It exists all right, Pete said. Day and night they let out that stink. Straight into my bedroom window. Just the job. Grin and bear it.
– Very congenial.
At Cambridge Heath station they went into a café and sat down with two teas.
– You know what? Pete said. I had one of my old boat dreams last night.
– Did you?
– Yes, Pete said. I was on this boat with Virginia, see? A motorboat. Going down a river. We turned a bend, and there, in front of us, about a hundred yards downstream, was the calmest patch of water you've ever seen. So I said to Ginny, we'll be all right when we get in there. I pressed the lever and we chugged on. Then all of a sudden the engine conked out. We'd run out of oil. I turned round, it was a bright day, and there was a police station standing on the bank. So I said, we'll get some in there. We managed to drift in, into a little nook. Then I turned to Virginia, and I said, wait a minute, before we go, we'd better have a look at your corpses. We went up to a little ledge, and lying there were two steel midgets, about a foot long, wrapped up in the firm's notepaper. Dead. We had a quick look at them and put them back. Then I went to get the oilcans, see? I

went down the steps and opened the door of the hatch. In the corner, lying against some sacking, were two Negro midgets, same size, made of steel, looking at me, staring, alive. I stared them out for a couple of minutes, then I said, don't think you're giving me a surprise. I knew you were there. I've had you taped from the kickoff.

– Christ, Mark said.

Pete grinned and picked his teeth with a matchstick.

Three

I should like to dance tonight. It is quite natural.

Virginia lay crouched on the sofa. The room was still. A shaft of sunlight fell across the carpet. There was no sound.

She stood up. The posture of the room changed. The sunlight jolted. The room settled. The sunlight re-formed. But, she thought, I stand upright and the balance is disturbed. I have thrown a spanner in the works. I have done violence to normally imperturbable forces. I have inflicted a reverse.

She smiled. It was a conceit, certainly, at which Pete would smile, and upon which he would certainly expand. What would he say? How would he begin? The room and the sunlight, he would say, were what they were, simply, and nothing more. There were many rooms and only one sun. A room might be faulty in idea and construction, and could be criticized from that point of view. A leak in the roof was a fault. An adequate room was proof of nothing but a builder's competence. It remained static until the house was pulled down; then, and then only, did it go through a process of drastic change; it did, in effect, cease to be a room. Change within a room while it stood was only to be located in the walls, the floor or the ceiling. Damp, warp, dryrot. Furniture, decoration, utilities, were merely incidental and, in some cases, nothing but impositions upon the room. To attribute bias or active desire to a room was merely the projection of a sick or deluded mind or the symptom of an emotional binge. To criticize the sun was absurd. The sun shone and the earth went round it. It was as impervious to criticism or to open revolt as it was to worship. It had no inclinations either way. Nor was it in any way productive to consider the sun as an opponent or ally, or relevant to your own actions as an interested force. It was not an interested force. It was the grossest intellectual falsehood to attribute to or impose upon the sun or a room any other concept or character. You could enjoy the sun or shut yourself from it. You could like a room or dislike it. You'd better watch your step, Virginia.

She laughed aloud. You'd better watch your step, Virginia. She looked across at the streetcorner, at which Pete would turn. But had she been fair? Had her essay at his manner of delivery, his way of stating a case, been accurate?

It was difficult to say. She had known him for two years, but was still unable to recollect his manner of speaking, from one day to another, without some measure of disbelief. Was it true that he spoke in that way? She could not but conclude that it was. Then, abruptly, it occurred to her that perhaps her disbelief was not disbelief at all, but simply a cloak for her apprehension.

If that was so, of what was she afraid? It had been that very power and conviction in his words which had first drawn her to him. They had met a week earlier in the library, and had spent two evenings together, walking. That day he had spoken to her on the telephone for the first time. My father is dead. Meet me for a cup of tea. They had met in a café in Hackney Road. The afternoon was close and pressing. As they sat down, Pete began to speak. She watched him, and listened. The police thought, he said, that his father had committed suicide. He himself did not think so. It was more likely he had been drunk and left the gas on. He had been mending the kitchen sink, there was something wrong with the pipe, when he heard his mother calling. She was in their room, standing over the body. His father was flat out on the carpet and the room full of gas. His mother had gone for the police. He had stayed there, with him. Had she ever been with a dead man? He was as dead as a bedpost and what was more, was nothing, absolutely nothing. He had felt as empty as an old sack. All this emotion business, what was it? A lot of bubbles blown down the coalhole. He was dry as an old faggot. The spanner was still in his hand. He could have easily gone back and finished mending the sink. Add two and two together and what did you have? Nothing. Before the police came he had stood for twenty minutes over the body. His father was as dead as a crusty old ant and, as for him, he couldn't give two pins to the dressmaker for the whole business.

Pete came in with a brown paper parcel under his arm and placed it on the table. He flapped the parcel open and took out a white summer dress, which he handed to her. She took off her sweater and skirt and changed into it.

– Stay still.

She stood, turning.

– Go to the window.

She walked to the window, held her skirt, turned, gazed at her reflection in the mirror.

– Like it? Stay where you are. The sun's down your sides and on your neck. You look lovely.

He sat down and lit a cigarette.

– It's beautiful, she said, sitting on the arm of his chair. Thank you.

– It suits you.

– I'll reserve it for special occasions.

– No, Pete said. Summer's the occasion for that dress. I want to see you walk in the air.

– In the sun.

– Yes. It was worth the doing.

– Where have you been?

– I went down to the Embankment. To watch the boats go by. A bit of quiet. It's like a monkeys' teaparty in that office.

– The girls?

– Yes.

– What do they do?

– I never look. Probably tickling each other in the vernacular. I keep well out of it.

– Do they let you?

– They don't come near me. They know I'd cut 'em into tripes.

– Was it hot today?

– Hot? I was mummified. The sea air did me good. Nice to watch the muck float.

Virginia walked to the mirror and looked at herself. She turned.

– Pete?
– Yes?
– What do you think of the sun?
– What do I what?
– How do you look upon the sun?
– What do you mean, how do I look upon it?
– No, it doesn't matter.
– No? What doesn't?

He strolled to the window.

– It's going down.
– I've been sitting here, she said.

He blew a smokering and watched it float in the air and flop.

– What do I think of the sun, eh? That's an interesting question.
– Did you enjoy making the dress?
– That dress? Sure.
– It's perfect.
– Yes. I moved a pawn with every stitch. It came off.

She joined him at the window.

– Would you like me to make you a petticoat? he asked.
– Yes, please.
– All right. I'll do that.

They watched the sun sinking between the chimneys. He leaned her temple to his, his arm about her waist.

– I like you today, he said.
– Because of the dress?
– No.

He turned her to him and kissed her.

– Let's have some tea.
– Yes.

He watched her move to the cupboard.

– Yes, he said, you look well in that dress.

- It's a masterpiece, she said.
- But you know what? he said, sitting down, in some ways you're more of a boy to me than a woman.
- What do you mean?
- No, you're a woman all right. But I like the way you conserve your mental energy. I can learn a lot from that, myself. But what you are, you're a good pal to me. You're a true companion.
- Really?
- Yes. You see, Mark, for instance, could never understand that. A woman is simply one thing to him and no more. A pregnancy of mind exists between us, which is outside his ken. Not all the time, perhaps, but a good deal of it.

She brought the cups to the table and poured milk.

- Mark wants all his women to call him sir and salute him three times a day. And he doesn't raise his hat for that one either. Another thing that niggles me is I'm sure he rides barebacked most of the time and doesn't give it a thought.
- Tea up.

They sat at the table and she cut into a loaf.

- You can't put a woman in a watertight compartment which you only open when the lights go out, Pete said. A woman has potential in other spheres.
- But you like him, don't you?
- Like him? Of course I like him.

He sliced a tomato and tipped salt on to his plate.

- He's a listener, Virginia said.
- He's a diehard. That's what he is. He was trying to convince me the other day that the answer to my problems was to go to bed with you more often.
- Mark?
- Yes.
- But how does he know? I mean, how does he know anything? About us?
- I don't know. I probably mentioned it to him.
- You mean you told him we don't make love very often?

27

- Yes.
- Oh.
- Why? Do you mind?
- No.
- It's hardly anything to be ashamed of.
- Yes, but why don't we write out a joint statement and send it to him?
- There's no need to do that, Pete said.

He poured the tea.

- To ease his mind.
- I don't think, Pete said, he's uncommonly disturbed about our problems.
- He may be, she said. He may be extremely concerned. Of course, I could always send him a poison-pen letter, telling him to mind his own bloody business.
- Hey, Pete said, wait a minute.
- Do we actually need his technical hints?
- Now hold on. First of all, you're talking about a friend of mine. Secondly, what he said you've heard entirely out of context, and thirdly, let's face it, there may be a grain of truth in it.
- Oh?
- Yes, Pete said, but you have to weigh that grain of truth against the case in hand. And – in a nutshell – I find it unsatisfactory as an overall working idea – in this particular case. Don't you? After all, a fuck is a fuck but it doesn't take place in a vacuum. The context is concrete.
- So's the fuck.
- That's beside the point, Pete said.

Four

There is the table. That is a table. There is the chair. There is the table. That is a bowl of fruit. There is the tablecloth. There are the curtains. There is no wind. There is the coalscuttle. There is no woman in this room. This is a room. There is the wallpaper, on the walls. There are six walls. Eight walls. An octagon. This room is an octagon, with no woman and one cat. There is the cat, on the carpet. Above the fireplace is a mirror. There are my shoes, on my feet. There is no wind. This is a journey and an ambush. This is the centre of the cold, a halt to the journey, and no ambush. This is the deep grass I hide in. This is the thicket in the centre of the night and the morning. There is the hundred-watt bulb like a dagger. It is neither night nor morning.

This room moves. This room is moving. It has moved. It has reached – a dead halt. There is no ambush. There is no enemy. There is no web. All's clear and abundant, not closed, not closing, not moved, not moving, having no stealth, possessing no guile. The time would be dark where there are gardens. Here are my stocks. This is my fixture. Perhaps a morning will arrive. If a morning arrives, it will not destroy my fixture, nor my luxury. Here are the paths on my walls, dead at their destination. A meetingplace for the sundries, all within harness. If it is dark in the night or light, nothing obtrudes. I have my cell. I have my compartment. All is ordered, in its place, no error has been made. I am wedged. There is no hiding. It is not night, nor is it morning. There is no ambush, only this posture, between two strangers, here is my fixture, here is my arrangement, when I am at home, when I am alone, not needing to arrange, I have my allies, I have my objects, I have my cat, I have my carpet, I have my land, this is a kingdom, there is no betrayal, there is no trust, there is no journey, they make no hole in my side.

They make a hole, in my side.

The bell split in the room. Len rose. He pushed aside books on the table, lifted the tablecloth, nudged the cat aside, and stood still. He felt deep into the body of the armchair, lifted the cushions, tapped along the windowsill, pulled the curtains to and stood still. The bell rang. He inspected the mantelpiece and knelt down to examine the hearth, crawled under the table and found the floor bare. He stood up and still. The bell rang. He moved to the dresser and emptied a bowl of letters, lifted a cup from its saucer and, shuddering, looked down at his feet. His eye caught a reflection, his chin drew in further. In the top pocket of his jacket were his glasses. He put them on, walked up the stairs to the front door and opened it.

– What were you doing? Mark asked, a wardance? I could see your shadow bobbing up and down.
– How could you see my shadow?
– Through the letterbox.
In the street, the rain slipped through the darkness.
– What did you say the time was? Len asked.
– Well, Mark said, it'd be getting on for that.
– You'd better come in.
In the room Mark took off his raincoat and sat heavily in the armchair, arranging the cushions.
– What's this, a suit? Where's your carnation?
– What do you think of it? Mark asked.
Len fingered the lapels, opened the jacket and looked inside.
– It's not a shmatta, he said.
– It's got a zip at the hips.
– A zip at the hips? What for?
– Instead of a buckle. It's neat.
– Neat? I should say it's neat.
– No turn-ups.
– I can see that. Why didn't you have turn-ups?
– It's smarter without turn-ups.
– Of course it's smarter without turn-ups.

- I didn't want it double-breasted.
- Double-breasted? Of course you couldn't have it double-breasted.
- What do you think of the cloth?
- The cloth? What a piece of cloth. What a piece of cloth. What a piece of cloth. What a piece of cloth. What a piece of cloth.
- You like the cloth?
- WHAT A PIECE OF CLOTH!
- What do you think of the cut?
- What do I think of the cut? The cut? The cut? What a cut! What a cut! I've never seen such a cut!

He sat down and groaned.

- Do you know where I've just been? Mark said.
- Where?
- Earls Court.
- Uuuuhh! What were you doing there? That's beside the point.
- What's the matter with Earls Court?
- It's a mortuary without a corpse.

Yawning, Len took off his glasses and pressed his knuckles to his eyes. Mark lit a cigarette and walked about the room, peering, his arm outstretched.

- What are you doing, dedicating a bull?
- That's right.

He found an ashtray and sat down.

- How did you get back, allnight bus?
- Of course.
- Which one?
- A 297 to Fleet Street. A 296 from there.

Len stood up to let the cat out the back door. He glanced outside and shut the door quickly.

- I can get you from Notting Hill Gate to here in an hour to the minute, he said.
- You can get *me*?
- It's simple. Perfect. Any time of the night. Say you're at

Notting Hill Gate at 1:52, no, it's Shepherds Bush at 1:52, say you're at Notting Hill Gate at 1:56 or 1:57, you can catch a 289 which gets to Marble Arch at about 2:05, or 6, about 2:06 and there, before you know where you are, you can pick up a 291 or 294, coming from the Edgware Road, gets to Marble Arch about 2:07. What did I say? That's right. That's it. You catch that to the Aldwych, gets there about 2:15 or 14 and at 2:16 you can pick up the 296 from Waterloo, takes you all the way to Hackney. If it's after three o'clock you can do the whole lot on a workman's ticket.

– Thanks very much, Mark said. What are you doing at Notting Hill Gate?

– Notting Hill Gate? That was for your benefit. I never go anywhere near Notting Hill Gate.

– I've just told you I was at Earls Court.

– Ah! said Len. Don't mention that place!

Mark scratched himself in the groin and stretched his legs.

– What were you doing, he asked, when I knocked on your door?

– Doing? Thinking.

– What about?

– Nothing. It was about nothing. This room. Nothing. A waste of time the thought and the thinking.

– What's the matter with this room?

– What's the matter with it? It doesn't exist! What you don't understand, you see, is that they're holding me up for ransom. If someone doesn't pay up quick I'm a dead duck.

– Are they asking much?

– They don't want currency. They don't want currency, they won't touch it. They're asking for something nobody's prepared to give. And I can't give it myself, because I haven't got it. Ah, that doesn't matter. What does it matter? There's a time and place for everything. These things should be faced.

– You never said a truer word.

- What? What do you mean by that?
- There's a time and place for everything. These things should be faced.
- You never said a truer word.

Mark coughed shortly and spat into the grate.

- I see that butter's going up, Mark said, wiping his mouth.
- I'm prepared to believe it, said Len, but it doesn't answer my question.
- What was that?
- What are you doing here? What do you want here?
- I thought you might give me a piece of bread and honey.

Len moved to the window and straightened a curtain.

- I know that you're frightened, you see.
- Oh yes? Mark said. What of?
- You're frightened that at any moment I'm liable to put a redhot burning coal in your mouth. Yes. But when the time comes, you see, what I should do is place the coal in my own mouth.
- Why's that?
- Why? That should be obvious. Pete would be able to tell you. He wouldn't be far out.
- Do you think so?
- He wouldn't be far out, Len said, sitting on the table. But I'll tell you something about him. As you're here. I know, you see, how things stand in the nothing. I know the nothing. The waste and dead air. But for Pete, even the nothing is something positive. Pete's nothing eats away, it's voracious, it's a malignant growth. But, can't you see, he fights back, he grapples to the death with it. He's a fighter. My nothing doesn't bother to act in such a way. It licks its paws while I shrink. It's a true nothing, a paralysis. There's no conflict, no battle. I am it. I am my own nothing. It's the only thing I have to rejoice in.
- Monkeynuts, Mark said.
- Why do you say that?
- Catpiss.

33

– All right, all right. If you believe that, I'll ask you another question.
– Ask.
– What have you got against Jesus Christ?
– That's a fast yorker.
– Can you play it?
– Which firm does he work for?
– He's a freelance.
– Oh yes, Mark said, he runs a book down at the dogs, doesn't he?
– He runs a book all right.
– That's the bloke, Mark said. Why? Has he put you on to any good things lately?
– He's given me a few hot tips, I can tell you that, Len said, and shrugged. Well, I suppose everyone's got a blind spot.
He began to stride the room, gripping and relaxing his fingers.
– As a matter of fact, Mark said, I did hear a rumour that your fares were going up.
Len stopped in his tracks and turned.
– Going up? Who told you that?
– I hope you're not going to strain the budget.
Len sat down, facing Mark at the fireplace, and smiled.
– I was waiting for this, he said.
– You might give me an idea of the fare stages. I could walk to save the extra penny.
– Listen here. I admit my prices are tending to go up, but if you feel you're unable to pay my costs I can always arrange to put you next to the driver or in the luggageboot. But, quite frankly, I'd much rather you give the correct fare. What do you want? But how did you know they were going up?
– Pete told me.
– Naturally.
– Why? Has he got money in it?
– In a way I suppose he has, but that's beside my point. I

can't see me getting the correct fare out of you or anything like it. But you must understand that I'm subject to the rise and fall of the balancesheets. If the market drops, or goes up, what can I do? Look here, Mark, it's quite true. My examiner is hiding behind a large book at the moment. I won't deny it. It's over there, by the wireless.

Mark turned in his chair and looked over his shoulder.

– A black book?
– Yes.
– A thick black book?
– Yes.
– Looks familiar.
– Huh.
– Lots of pages, in that book.
– Yes. Well, he's hiding there, but I mean to see him, I can tell you that. I mean to have a look at him, at least.
– What's wrong with that? Mark said.
– Nothing. There's nothing wrong with that. I'll let you know the result of my investigations.
– All right.
– But, Mark, you can do me a favour and don't spit. You don't have to spit. I know you've got Droit, but so have I. You must have manners, even if you've got nothing else. All I ask is, use restraint.
– Hold on a minute. Who's raising the fares, me or you?
– Let me explain, Len said. You see, one of my troubles is that I tend to mistake the reflections of the palace and the moon for the real objects. My ancestors tell me which are the real objects and I respect age. But I must find out for certain myself. I must try to look through the reflections and find the object. What can I lose? Of course, you have your Droit, but let me have my Droit and you can have your Droit!
– Howzat?
– Not out.
– What about Pete? Can he have his Droit too?
– Pete'll have his Droit, Len said, when we're dead and

buried. Pete has his Droit whether you like it or not.

Mark lit a cigarette and blew the match.

- Listen, Len, he said, all you've got to do is put up a notice: Spitting Prohibited. Who could argue with that? The fare's high enough. I couldn't afford to pay a fine on top of it.
- Yes, that's a good idea. I'll do that. But if you do happen to let out a spit and you can't pay the fine, I won't be responsible for the consequences.
- The question won't arise.
- But you can see. Can't you see that I must put up my own fares and travel in the front seat so that I won't have to ride in my own luggageboot? I can't see from there, and I must keep my eye on the driving. There'll be plenty of room for me because hardly anyone else can afford the price. In that case I can keep to my own route and avoid traffic jams. I must do that.

Five

Pete looked over her body to the humped shadows of the room and then, gathering her hair, he smoothed it back upon the cushion. About the windowframe the moon edged. She inclined him towards her. He rested his head on her breasts. Above them, through the open window, a light breeze moved. She looked past his head to the walls. She could not distinguish their meetingplace. They seemed at once distant and close upon her. She stared up at the creased ceiling. The pale rim of the hanging shade, at first apparent, now in her sight faded, changing from form into shape into the bulge of the ceiling. Upon a wall, an oblong of barred reflection angled from light in the window. The darkness pointed upon their bodies, weighted, and as she stared it out, dispersed, withdrawing.

– I have banished darkness from the face of the earth, she said.

Pete stretched his arms around a chairleg, and clasped his hands.

– How did you do that?

– No, it is dark, she said. More so since you moved.

– It's the heat. If it weren't so hot it wouldn't be so dark.

– But in summer, Virginia said, day doesn't become night. The day is the day. In winter, the night's in the day. In summer –

– I'm not quite sure, Pete said, that I agree with you.

He yawned and stretched, pressing the fender with his foot.

– But it is dark now. Darker because we're so white, she said.

– Yes.

He pulled her to him and kissed her, turning her on to the cushions, and stared down at her face.

– You don't close your eyes.

– No, she said.

– Why not?

– I want to see you.

– Why?

– Because I love you.

– Yes, said Pete, so do I.

The moon had gained the body of the window. Between the bars of a chair, it shone down on them.

– Listen. Don't you believe I love you?

– Do you?

– Do you believe it?

– No.

– You're wrong, Pete said. I love you.

He reached up to the chairside and drew two cigarettes from his jacket, lit them and placed one in her mouth.

– In some ways I'm very backward.

He allowed the smoke to collect and divided it with a breath.

– But I'm becoming less ignorant.

– Ignorant?

– I think I'm learning to love you.

– How?

– Perhaps you're teaching me. Who else could?

– Me?

– Who else?

She sat up and faced him.

– The other day you told me I was like a boy to you.

– I said in some ways.

– But –

– I've been thinking.

– What?

– I've been doing some thinking.

He dropped his head to the cushion at her hip, stretching his legs to the hearth and she, swivelling with him, looked down. Bending, she kissed him, and then moved away to sit upright. He pulled her back and pressed his mouth to her shoulder. Her hair swung across his face. He kissed her breasts. She stared at the window. The light was glazed. She turned on her hip and fell against his body. His arms enfolding her, they kissed, rolling off the cushions. His thigh was closed between her own. They were still, the underside of the table black above them, her hands at his waist. She moved her hands along his body. He loosed himself from the embrace and sat up.

– Yes, you're very beautiful.

They moved back to the cushions and faced each other sitting.

– But what was I saying? he smiled.

– You were thinking.

– Yes.

– You had been thinking.

Pete picked up her cigarette from the hearth and passed it to her.

– What happens sometimes, he said, is that you have, in fact, proceeded farther than your thought. You're behind your own times and you don't know it. All this, I see now, has been happening in me for some time and I haven't been sufficiently aware of it. Or perhaps I was reluctant to trust it. I've been learning to love you for some time.

Virginia was silent. He lay back and gazed into the dark corner of the room.

– Are you sure?

– No. But I want to be. I want you to help me prove it.

– Yes.

– We can do it. I'm sure of that.

– I can't hear a sound, said Virginia.

– Hey.

– Yes?

– I'm going to stay here tonight.

– You are?

– Yes.

– I can't remember when you last did that.

– Well, he said, there you are.

– Here I am and here you are. Would you like to dance with me?

- What do you mean? Now?
- Yes.
- Not at the moment, eh? Pete said.
- All right.
- Let's have some wine.

He stood up, walked to the table, poured two glasses of red wine.

- You're very slim, very tight.
- Cheers.
- The moon's following you about.
- No, I'm getting in its way.
- That's your privilege.
- Yes, why not?

He stood at the window, looking out.

- There's no wind.
- Len once said that to me, she said.
- What?
- He just looked at me and he said, there's no wind.
- Ah, said Pete. Len. I'm going to see him tomorrow night.

He bent his head and looked up at the sky.

- All quiet up there, anyway.
- Sounds very grave, she said.
- What does?
- Going to see Len tomorrow night.
- No. Why?

He sat down by her.

- What are we, you and me? What we are not is items in a double lovemachine.
- No. We're certainly not that.
- Quite. You represent for me something much more than that. For example, you don't need to clutter yourself up with ornaments of provocation, that kind of stuff. They're beside the point. Your provocation is of another sort, it's of a purer sort. Your loveliness is of another sort.
- Is it?
- Yes. It exists in spite of yourself and everyone else. You

40

don't have to go in for titillation, like the rest of them. That's
not your vocation. Your vocation is to be a disciple of the
Gods. Do you follow me?

Pete emptied the bottle into their glasses. Virginia slipped into
bed.

– Did I ever tell you what my bugbear was when I used to
knock about with Mark – in the days I was one of the boys?
Pete said. Armourplated women. It's one stage less difficult
than making love to a crowbar. I remember once a suspender
snapped. We were sitting on a tombstone in Hackney grave-
yard. I was caught between the buckle and the other
machinery. I nearly had a penis stricture. She was a nurse,
that one. Fully qualified. She used to pinch me on the
epidermis to show how she would lay me out as a corpse.
Very entertaining, but all in all a mug's game.

– Did you and Mark always go about together then?
– Yes. Shift work. Work. Work tomorrow, he said, yawning.
Do you know that in the firm's cellar there's enough venison
to sink a ship?

– Who's it for?
– The directors and the directors' wives.

He climbed into the bed and held her in his arms.

– This is good for me, she said.
– For me too.
– It's not right for a schoolteacher to sleep alone all the time.

A churchbell struck two.

– Your eyes are very bright, she said.
– I've never seen yours so wide.
– Mine grow at night.

He traced her brows and the hollows of her eyes, and her cheeks.

– I wonder if I'll dream tonight.
– No, she murmured, her eyes closed, we won't dream.
– Look, Pete said, at the moon.

Leaning forward, they looked through the window.

– Yes.

Bordered by ribs and caves of cloud the bright moon stuck.

Six

- Whatever you do, don't wake the cat up.
- Do me a favour.
- You don't understand. Today I was playing Bach to that cat. I was trying a sonata for unaccompanied violin. Can't you see? He deserves a rest, from his point of view. Not, I can tell you this, that I pretend to understand his point of view. Though I'm closer to that cat than you might think. We've a lot in common.
- Dear oh dear, Pete said.

Len turned the key in the door. They walked down to the living room. The cat, lying on the armchair, lifted its head.

- He's awake.
- He'll never sleep again, Pete said, sitting down. Bach may be the making of you, but he's the ruination of that cat.
- I can't see that, Len said.

He nudged the cat from the chair. It dropped with a thump and stared, switching its tail, at Pete.

- You may not understand his point of view, but I think he understands mine well enough.
- You mean in respect of him?
- Yes.
- What is it?
- Scorn, Pete said, and defiance. Slight regard, contempt, and anything that may not misbecome the mighty sender, do I prize him at.
- That's sad. Good God.
- Look here. Any sensible man would be cagey of a cat who was mathematical and musical and proclaimed himself, on those grounds, king of the roost.
- Did you say cagey or leery?

- I said cagey.
- I thought you said leery.

The cat sat down on the carpet and licked its paws.

- That cat has ceased to be the animal he was, Pete said. Look at him. He's become a semiquaver.
- You can't lay everything at Bach's door.
- Why not? He rules this house with a rod of iron.

Len shook his head and drew the curtains. Shaking his head, he sat on the table, drawing breath between his clenched teeth. He lowered his glasses and stared up over the rim, about the room, eventually twitching them back to their level.

- What? he exclaimed, whipping the glasses from his nose. What was that? What did you say? Eh? Bach? Bach? What about Bach?

Pete lay back in the armchair.

- Tell me something, he said. Who was Bach?
- Who was he? You can't ask me a question like that!
- What can you tell me about him?
- You're mad.
- Look, Pete said, leaning forward, have a bit of common. You must know something about him, after all this barney. What was he up to?
- No, Len said. Ask someone else. I can't tell you. It's out of the question. I can't speak about him.
- No?

Len shrugged and opened the cupboard door. From a shelf he took a bottle of wine, drew the cork and sniffed, placed the bottle on the table, with two glasses. He glared at the bottle, lifted it up and read the label. He then passed it to Pete. Pete sniffed and passed it back. Len raised his glasses and held his breath to sniff again. He poured the wine, lifted the glass to his nose, looked into it, and took a quick sip. Keeping the wine in his mouth he walked about the room, rolling his eyes and flicking his eyelids. He began to gargle.

- Bach? he said, spitting the wine back into the glass, it's simple. The point about Bach – the point about Bach –

43

He lifted the bottle, frowned, and put it back in the cupboard, closing the door.

– The point, Len said, about Bach, is that – give me a chance – is that –

He sat on the table and stood hurriedly, picking up the glass and slapping the seat of his trousers, on which the spilt wine clung.

– Ugh! Ugh! Ugh!

– Use a rag.

– Ugh!

– Turn round, Pete said. There's nothing there.

– I'm wet through.

– You were talking about Bach.

Len undid his trousers and stepped out of them. He grasped them by the legs and shook them violently. He examined the stain, stepped into them and did them up.

– Thirty-nine and six five years ago.

– Why don't you stand on your head next? Pete said. What about, for Christsake get on with it, bloody Bach?

– Bach? It's simple. The only point about Bach is that he saw his music as emanating through him and not from him. From A via Bach to C. There's nothing else to say.

He sat in an armchair and leaned back.

– Look at Beethoven.

– What do you mean?

– What do you mean? Len said. Beethoven is always Beethoven. Bach is like cold or heat or water or flame. He is Bach but he's not Bach. There's no comparison.

– Wait a minute –

– Look, Len said, feeling the cloth under his buttocks, when I listen to Bach's music I know what recognition is. Not recognition that I am listening to Bach – just recognition. There's no skin, there's no wood, there's no flesh, there's no bone, there's no orgasm, there's no recovery. There's no life, but there's no death. There's no deed. Consciousness is left to the four breezes, or the forty, of course, it depends who you are.

– Does it?

– There is no question of saying – It is here, now. That doesn't apply. It would apply if Bach were someone else. Then you could say – Yes, I am listening to this – I. But Bach doesn't want to know you. It's a pointless attitude. Pointless.

– Yes.

– Bach is the composer for the weak. But also for the strong, in that he is terrifying to many who are neither weak nor strong.

– Whoah!

– Bach, Len said, standing up and walking to the wall, is not concerned with murder, nature, massacre, earthquake, plague, rebellion, famine or the other one. He is not concerned with *big things*, as such. There is always room for him. You can, you can believe this or not, you can put him in your back pocket. You can put him in your back pocket. But if you put him in your back pocket, you're not putting *him* in your back pocket, you must understand that.

– Huh.

– They tell me, Pete, Len said, sitting on the table, that a warm and generous woman makes all else pale into insignificance. No doubt at all. Even Shakespeare becomes a few well-chosen words. But Bach could never become, for me, a few well-chosen notes. I suppose that's because I distrust everyone. I can understand, I think, where my property becomes a woman's too and all is forgetfulness. But the last card of all, at the moment, is his.

– I see.

– One, you see, Len said, standing, purely technical point about Bach is his insistence and his flowering justification of that insistence. Bu bu bu bu bu bu bu bu bu bu bu b bu bu bu bu bu bu bu bu bu bu bu..........bu tillellellellellalalalalala bu bu bu etcetera. You can come in on the tillellella, but you can easily fit in the previous bu bus. No trouble. That's all I've got to say about Bach. There you are. You shouldn't have asked me.

– Well, said Pete. Ah. Yes, you've told me something.

They stood with their hands in their pockets, on the carpet.

– What about a cup of cocoa?

– Cocoa?

– Yes, Pete said, we'll drink a toast.

– All right. All right, I don't mind doing that.

They left the room and walked down to the scullery, the cat following. Through the basement window, the moon shone crooked on the hanging crockery. Len switched on the light and put the kettle on. He brought out a tin of cocoa.

– Yes, you've got something there.

– It's not possible.

– My face is a death's head, Pete said, looking into the flaked mirror above the sink.

– You're quite right.

– Do you know, a neighbour stopped me the other day and told me I was the handsomest man she'd ever seen.

– What did you say to that?

– What could I say?

– I've got a few bagels, Len said.

Pete sat at the table and stroked its surface.

– This is a very solid table.

– I said I've got some bagels.

– No thanks. How long have you had this table?

– It's a family heirloom.

– Yes, said Pete, leaning back, I'd like a good table, and a good chair. Solid stuff. Made for the bearer. I'd put them in a boat. Sail it down the river. A houseboat. You could sit in the cabin and look out at the water.

– Who'd be steering?

– You could park it. Park it. There's not a soul in sight.

– Where would you go?

– Go? Pete said. You wouldn't go.

– Here's your cocoa.

They sipped.

– How's Mark?

46

- Fine, Len shrugged.
- What does he have to say for himself?
- He said he wouldn't spit last night.
- I'm glad to hear it.
- I'm glad to be able to say it.
- What's he got to spit about?
- Well, he likes a good spit sometimes.
- Yes, but what's he spitting, or not spitting, about, this time?
  Pete asked.
- My examiner.
- Who?
- Christ. Jesus Christ.
- What, Pete said, sitting up, is he thinking of having a gob at
  Jesus Christ?
- Not exactly. But he can't help it now and again, I suppose.
- What are you gabbling about?
- Well, Len said, you told him yourself I was having a look at
  the New Testament.
- Oh. So he's spitting at that, eh?
- I told you, he said he wouldn't.
- That's very generous of him.
- Well, he may be in a position to. You can never tell.
Pete dug his hands in his pockets and laughed.
- You're talking like Joe Doakes. In a position to spit at Jesus
  Christ? I'll split a gut in a minute. But go on, I'm interested.
  Tell me. Why do you think he's in a position to spit?
- You're tearing my fingernails off, one by one.
- I'm letting you off lightly. Come on.
- All right. I think he has one answer, that's all. Even if he
  hasn't, I think I think he has, and even if I don't think he has
  he may have or, if you like, someone with his name may
  have.
- Someone with his name may have! You've made the cat crawl
  under the table. Is this how you talk to the cat every night?
- All right, Len said. You've got something to say. Why don't
  you say it?

47

- No, Pete said.

He picked up his cup and gulped.

- No, he smiled. I've got nothing to say.
- Really? Len frowned.

He looked up and shook his head and then, reflecting, began to chuckle.

- All right. He said something else though, that I'm sure you'll appreciate.
- What's that?
- He was talking about Dean Swift, you see, and he said he ended up eating his own shit and left his money to lunatic asylums. Have you seen Pete lately? Just like that. Straight off. What do you think of that?

Pete sat forward and laughed.

- That's very amusing.
- Amusing! I should say it is.
- Yes, very odd.
- Odd? What do you mean, odd?
- When I got home from work the other day, Pete said, a neighbour was at the door. Smoke was coming through the window.
- What?
- It was all right. It was a cake I'd forgotten about, in the oven. The place was intact, but the cake was just about ready for your cat. The neighbour, though, was in a state, white in the face. Obviously thought I'd been boiling human bones.
- Yes, I can see that, Len nodded.
- You can?
- Oh yes, I can see that all right.

The tap dripped. Len turned it tight.

- Well, how are you, Len? Pete said.
- What?
- How's things?
- Huh, Len said, and kicked a chair. I'm supper for the crows.

- Who is?
- I'll tell you, Len said, and straddled the chair. I'm a non-participator.
- Go home. You? You're just a Charley Hunt.
- That too.
- I'll tell you what your trouble is, Pete said. You need to be more elastic.
- Elastic? Elastic. You're quite right. Elastic. What are you talking about?
- How are you getting on with Christ?
- Christ? No, no. No. He's what he is and I'm what I'm not. I don't see how we can be related.
- Giving up the ghost, Pete said, lighting a cigarette, isn't so much a failure as a tactical error. By elastic I mean being prepared for your own deviations. You don't know where you're going to come out next at the moment. You're like a rotten old shirt. Buck your ideas up. They'll lock you up before you're much older, if you go on like this. You want to cut out this terror and pity lark. It's bullshit. Commonsense can work wonders. The first thing you've got to do is kill that cat. It's leading you nowhere.

Len stood up and wiped his glasses. He looked down, shivering.

- No, he said. There is a different sky each time I look. The clouds run about in my eye. I can't do it.
- The apprehension of experience, Pete said, must obviously be dependent upon discrimination if it is to be considered valuable. That's what you lack. You haven't got the faculty for making a simple distinction between one thing and another. Every time you walk out of this door you go straight over a cliff. What you've got to do is nourish the power of assessment. How can you hope to assess and verify anything if you walk about with your nose stuck between your feet all day long?
- Look, Len said, I could never give up Bach.
- Who asked you to do that?

49

– No? Oh. Oh, I see. I misunderstood you.
– What?
– You didn't ask me to give up Bach?
– What are you talking about?
– It must have been somebody else.

Len cleared the cups and put them in the sink.

– I wonder what Mark's up to.
– Saying sweet syllables into some lady's earhole, Pete smiled. Don't you think?
– Probably.
– Yes, Pete said, he's a strange chap, is Mark. I sometimes think he's a man of weeds.

Balancing the chair under his body, he put his legs up on the table.

– Yes, he said, I sometimes think he's a man of weeds. And yet I don't know. He surprises me, that bloke, now and again, for the good, I mean. But often I wonder about him. I sometimes think he makes capital out of the mud on his shoes, that he's just playing a game. But what game?

Len turned the tap and rinsed a saucer.

– I wonder, Pete said, now and again, why I bother. He's got, after all, a conceit enough to hid an army in. And what's there to back it up? There's the point. Eh?

Len rinsed a cup and did not answer.

– An attitude. But has it substance or is it barren? Sometimes I think it is barren, as barren as a bombed site. But I won't be dogmatic on it.
– No, Len said, wiping the cups.
– He's an elusive customer. Of course, I like him, when it comes down to it. You can forgive a lot. But he's never done a day's work in his life, that's his trouble. He's a bit of a ponce, he wouldn't deny it. But I think he overdoes the lechery. Between you and me, he'll be a spent force in no time if he doesn't watch his step.
– Pss! Pss! Len hissed.

The cat slid out from under the table. Len, warding it off,

poured milk into a saucer and stood up. The cat lapped.

- What do you call that cat?
- Solomon, said Len.

He leaned against the sideboard and poked at the corner of his eye, under his glasses.

- Here, Pete said, I'll tell you a dream I had last night, if you like, to cheer you up.
- All right.
- I didn't expect to dream last night.
- What was it?
- It was very straightforward, Pete said. I was with Virginia in a tube station, on the platform. People were rushing about. There was some sort of panic. When I looked round, I saw everyone's faces were peeling, blotched, blistered. People were screaming, booming down the tunnels. There was a firebell clanging. When I looked at Ginny, I saw that her face was coming off in slabs too. Like plaster. Black scabs and stains. The skin was dropping off like lumps of catsmeat. I could hear it sizzling on the electric rails. I pulled her by the arm to get her out of there. She wouldn't budge. She just stood there, with half a face, staring at me. I screamed at her to come away, but she still wouldn't move. Then I suddenly thought – Christ, what's my face like? Is that what she's staring at? Is that rotting too?

Len gasped.

- One for the black book, eh? Pete said.

Len covered his eyes with his hands.

- Doesn't matter about that, Pete said. Watch this. See how many I can do.
- What?
- Keep a count.

Pete lay stomach down on the floor and began to propel himself up and down, on his forearms. Len leaned forward, watching him.

- How many? Pete grunted.
- Fifteen.

Pete continued, staring in front of him.

– Twenty.

– Uh.

– Twenty-five.

– Uh.

– Twenty-nine.

– Enough.

He relaxed and grinned, sitting on the floor.

– Not bad, eh?

– What are you made of? Len said. It's beyond me.

– Give me a week and I'll do thirty-five.

Seven

The dwarfs are back on the job, Len said. They're keeping an eye on proceedings. They clock in very early, scenting the event. They are like kites in a city disguise; they only work in cities. However, they are certainly skilled labourers and their trade is not without risk. They wait for a smoke signal and unpack their kit. They are on the spot with no time wasted and circle the danger area. There, they take up positions, which they are able to change at a moment's notice, if necessary. But they don't stop work until the job in hand is ended, one way or another.

I have not been able to pay a subscription, but they have consented to take me into their gang, on a short term basis. My stay with them cannot be long. I can't see this particular assignment lasting into the winter. The game will be up by then. At present, however, this is the only way I myself can keep an eye on proceedings. And it is essential that I keep a close watch on the rate of exchange, on the rise and fall of the market. Probably neither Pete nor Mark is aware of the effect the state of his exchange has upon my market. But it is so.

And so I shall keep the dwarfs company and watch with them. They miss very little. With due warning from them I shall be able to clear my stocks, should there be a landslide.

Eight

At Pete's request she sat down. He had something to say, he explained, to which she would do well to listen, since it might prove fruitful. Standing on the hearth to begin, he invited her to consider the question of physical appearance and to what degree it was relevant. His own concern was with where the body ceased to be a positive force and became a liability. For example, there was himself and Mark. He would venture to say that their physical appearances went before them and established a contact before their personalities were inclined to participate. To the undiscerning, that might serve as a pointer to what was to come, but how far was that pointer accurate? He himself was a pretty boy, Mark looked as though he had just got out of, or was just getting into, bed. Both their appearances were, he hoped, inconsistent with the facts of the matter. It was, indeed, one of their few mutual problems. They were both obliged to come to some sort of working arrangement with their form in the flesh, and the course they took to resolve the question could be decisive. It seemed to him that Mark was quite content to conform to his body's disposition. He was satisfied to accept a worship based on those grounds alone. But he surely had more to offer than his profile and his abilities as a sexual mechanic. He was letting his potentialities slip. Acting in such complacent liaison with his body's whims, he could not hope to preserve any objective or critical point of view, either in relation to himself or to others. For a distance had always to be kept between what was smelt and your ability to weigh in the balance the located matter or event. Mark was not only failing in this but was a closed book to all emendation. He was not open to criticism.

She listened.

Len, of course, was not so much a physical type as a physical symptom. His behaviour, his manner of expression, were informed by something in the nature of a central and compulsive stammer. He was never still, or when he was, his stillness was both a gesture and an argument. But it was never his features themselves that were to the fore, it was what came after them; the smokescreens, the distress signals of his nature. He was encountered on that territory only and to comment on his physical make-up was irrelevant, for his body, as such, simply, did not participate. The constant activity one noted when in his company obtained only at the nerve ends and limits of his body, and to objects attached to it; his hands and his glasses. His eyes were active only as nerve ends, they could not be regarded as features. And where this nervous territory normally constituted a part of the sum, in Len's case it was the sum. It preceded his body, which was by way of being merely a conveyance for the box of tricks and conundrums he was.

She lay back.

In point of fact, Len preserved no more of a distance between what he smelt and what he thought about it than Mark, but for different reasons. They both failed to distinguish between any given smell and the conclusion consequent upon it, but where Mark was simply too lazy to attempt to differentiate, Len was too lacking in trust in his own discernment. He must stick to the smell and equate it with the thought, till the thought was the smell, because he was unable to face up to the true nature of thought and its demands. But while Mark was not open to correction, though he might in time discover his errors or be brought to appreciate them by example, Len was open both to instruction and to assistance.

She lay back, listening.

This, he went on, he was prepared to give, and more, to either of them. For upon consideration, taking all differences into account, he knew their friendship as valuable. In fact he was not sure whether they might not be said to constitute a church, of a kind. They were hardly one in dogma or direction,

55

but there was common ground and there was a framework. At their best they formed a unit, and a unit which, in his terms, was entitled to be called a church; an alliance of the three of them for the common good, and a faith in that alliance. It was, of course, a matter of working towards a balanced and flexible structure. He was well aware this structure was nowhere near completion. Their differences were conducive to corruption within the unit. Labour was needed to contain them, but if they were contained or, what was more productive, brought to an honest reconcilement, then they would be able to speak of achievement. For him the effort was worthwhile. It was more than worthwhile, it was quite frankly, essential. It was the simple matter of communication. If he remained unable to communicate with his fellowman there was nothing left but dryrot.

She listened.

Having admitted the possibility of corruption within the unit, he would deal with the question of corruption from outside it. An outside influence, he was convinced, could be absorbed without harm. For instance, Virginia was acting upon one of them at that moment; himself. On the assumption that she did him positive good, he himself would have more to offer the church. If, on the other hand, she were doing him positive harm, he took it the others would fulfil their obligations towards him, by way of understanding. A case, of course, could be made for an outside influence acting, say, on Len in one way, and on Mark in another, so as to cause dissension between them and corrupt the fabric. But in that event it would be simply a matter of choice. They would have to consider which was of more value; the subject of their quarrel, or their alliance. In such a case, either the church would profit or they could all pack up and go home.

The day becoming twilight, she eased herself in the chair, the room's shades meeting, till now, words again, about her, from the bed, where he squatted, smoking.

The empty and the quack, he had had his fill of them. His way of life had forced a crisis. His time spent, for instance, in the

Church of England, had been a waste and a delusion. It had been nothing but intellectual dishwashing, where he had deceived himself he was putting in spadework as a positive visionary. It had served only as a degradation of his powers. His potentialities were wearing thin, becoming stagnant, out of nothing but disaffection at continually remaining potential. Beyond his own resources, he would be frank, he had little. The time was to do. He was, however, condemned to a course, of that let there be no doubt. He must work his disease to the bone and so cure it. His condition could be destroyed only by fulfilling it, to that he was reconciled. But to remain a part of the Church of England required a kind of patience he no longer possessed. They were too far drowned in inanities. For instance, their idea of the nature of God was an impertinence. All they were in fact doing was patting themselves on the back. As for God, they had given him his hat and told him to wait. They looked upon him as their creation; a commodity. They were directing the firm and all he had to do was run the errands. God did the donkeywork; they reaped the profits. At the last meeting he had attended he had declared: Where is this God of yours? Put him down here on the table and let's have a look at him. Let's all have a butcher's. They thought a bomb had burst. In reality, they were the kind of people, who, if the gates of heaven opened to them, all they would feel would be a draught.

In the dusk she sat still. Now Pete drew near to her.

The same thing applied to the poets. They were guilty of a criminal defection. He must impress upon her that the act of writing was the act of committing yourself to yourself. Consequently it was a moral question. The poets about them were signing their own death warrant each time they signed their name. Their work was not selfexpression so much as self-creation. And all that issued forth was a lie. Each poem they wrote was nothing more than a posthumous fart. The labour of dead men, who could only give birth to a corpse, in their own image. It was a debasement and sellout of the purpose of writing, active only in that it delighted in its own smell. It was fatal for a work of art to be conceived and brought about in a vacuum. It had to be purposive in the same way as a piece of cooking. What did you make a plumpudding for if you weren't going to eat it? For, besides being selfcommittal, writing was bound to inform, enlighten and perhaps transform. Man might be an error of judgement but as yet he remained a relevant factor. And these people were relevant only in that they were a constant reminder of the mental waxwork he was faced with. They committed a sin with every word they wrote.

It was dark. Virginia rose and put the kettle on the gas. Later, they went for a walk across the Lea.

Nine

Pete sauntered into Threadneedle Street, blinked the grey bending stone, stopped. He looked up.

> Valparaiso Bank. Must be Valparaiso Bank. Building without bricks. Geometric, brickless. An act of faith. Straight as a dye. Up to the top and back. Geometric conversations with the sun. A slant on the holy rood. The sun's angle angled, made into commerce. Taken down in shorthand. Don't be deceived by deceptive reflections. Pneumonic irrelevances. There's a glut on the market. Worse than a periphrastic conjugation. But the sun all shapes and sizes. Making mischief. Doubletalk on the roofs. Signlanguage. What's that? A dihedron? Or who spat on the polygon? Throw me the mathematical ball. I'm inclined to believe it.

He leaned against the wall.

> Light a cigarette and look normal.

Down brickless Valparaiso Bank the sun strained, lanced, stuck on the flagpole. Drawing smoke, Pete viewed the trafficpress, the grate and bout of noonday vehicles; the sinking figures in the glare, passing, stepping; the needleshiver in the sunstreet. A quick black arm pushed swerving past.

> Look. Yes. Linseed and sealingwax. Stiffcollared puppydog. Lightweight. Bouncy on the balls of his feet. Rulers of a nation. The inside story. Masons and makers of the peace. Hot tips off the cuff. See you all right. Nothing but the best. Password and a nifty gin. What's your name and number? Keep it.

Leaning, he surveyed the pacing street. The fitted buildings poised backwards, out of their incline. They halted between sun and sun.

Near siesta time. Flat out on the roofgarden. Lemontea and a canopy. In the shade of the old appletree. Out of the draught. Turn the globe and pick your teeth.

Hundreds of windows and not a face at any of them. Day doesn't exist. Underground work. Getting on with the job. An eighthour day with no day in it. The working world. Where I labour and trespass. At whose direction? Who spoke, saying. Don't believe a word of it.

Pete turned about, looked up. Valparaiso Bank windows winked anonymous glint.

Glinting from big toe to earhole. All done by anon. Depends if you have the tools. Plenty of work for all. But no permit without God's grace. Frame it. Dust it in all weathers, all days.

Building wavering, and the next, and the next, along Threadneedle Street.

What's this? Proudly tripping. Would she say no? Look at those flanks. Wim wam. Strap me and buy one. Wam wim. She'd ride a cockhorse. All the way to Dalston. Don't doubt it. Been there before. Left by the frontdoor. Without my roe, like a dried herring.

– Peter Cox! Good lord!

Retribution.

– Well, well, well!

– Derek! Pete greeted, handgripping. Well, well.

– Ha-ha, beamed Derek, handpulling, well, well!

– Well, Pete smiled. What are you doing around here?

– I work here, laughed Derek, his face shining.

– No? said Pete. I wouldn't have believed it. So do I.

– No? gleamed Derek, his face spreading. I would never have dreamt it. Well, well, well! Where?

– Where? Pete said. Oh, Dobbin and Laver. Round the corner.

– I'm your neighbour! rammed Derek, his face breaking, shoulderbanging.

– Well! said Pete. Well, well, well.

- You look in the pink, cheered Derek, his face folding. Haven't changed a bit. Still got your curly locks, eh? How are you getting on? Good job?
- Oh, Pete skidded, shrugging, it's – you know – not – bad – Derek, old man.
- Good grief! clamped Derek, his face shutting. It must be three years since we met! And before that, not since we left school.
- Yes, Pete said, there's something in that.
- My God! snored Derek, his face foaming, it's a century! What are you doing now? Lunch hour?
- Well, yes, huffed Pete, it is. More or less.
- What a bit of luck! hammed Derek, his face scalding. What about a drink?
- Well, actually, creased Pete, I'm rushing off to meet a bloke. Mark Gilbert. You knew him, didn't you?
- Gilbert! Of course! mooed Derek, his face grinding. Went on the stage, didn't he?
- Well, yes, Pete said, but you see, he's got something on his mind, I think. Wants to have a quiet chat with me about it. You know how it is, Derek. You know these actors, eh?
- Women trouble, eh? parried Derek, his face flaking. I know what you mean all right. Actor, eh?
- Yes, Pete said, they're a funny lot. It's a shame but there it is. But we're sure to bump into each other. Both working around here, like.
- I should hope so! slammed Derek, his face singing, elbow-gripping. We must have a drink after all these years.
- Without a doubt.
- Well, look here, Peter, vaulted Derek, his face chanting, back-slapping, why don't you give me a ring? We can meet one night after work. Wait a minute, I'll write it down. I still see Robin and Bill, you know? Ever see any of the old crowd? Oh yes, Gilbert. Here you are. Well, look, give me a ring, will you? And I'll ring up Robin and Bill, and we can all have a jolly good yarn.

61

– How's Robin these days?

– Blooming, old boy. Not married yet. You married yet? sharped Derek, his face sprouting.

– Ha-ha, said Pete. Oh, that's it, is it? Good. I'll do that then. Must toddle now. You know these actors.

– Grand luck meeting you! chucked Derek, his face ceasing. Don't forget.

Pete turned, waved, and crossed the road.

> Sweating all over. Someone arranged that. Must keep my eyes open. Wouldn't have seen me on the other side. Shady. Oh yes he would. They all do. Should wear a hat. Grow a moustache. Get a wheelchair. False nose can work wonders. That was a close one. Where's that piece of paper. Uh. Down the drain.

Between hoots and carshins Pete crossed the road. Under planes of corrugated iron he saw bricks and pans arranged and raised by figures in heat. He turned into a sidestreet.

> Down here. River. Yes. Cooler the nearer you sniff. Hum still though. Hum and crackle. London burning. Look. Sandwich girls. Legshow for a city gent. Wall perchers. Waiting for a catch. Birds of prey. What's it like to be a woman, Maisie? I wouldn't know. Nothing to get in your way. No hang and no jut. Smooth and wet. Fingers in the paper. Tissuepaper for all purposes. Lipstick and cucumber. Eyes. No I'm not coming your way. And never's the word. Some of them like it sweaty. Animal labour. Putrefied mechanics. Barebacked with a squelch. In God's image. Costs nothing. Not good enough. Sluttery to neat excellence opposed. Sweat and spit and nothing to show. The act of mercy. Eachway bet. Money or your life. Something for nothing. The general levelling. Not like that. Not like that.

> There's a boat. One for me. That's a good boat. Boats. Midgets. Take a butcher's at that sun. Bloodthirsty. Sails. Midgets. Drivelling midgets. Sun is steel too. Quite steel. If

I were steel. All problems solved. Ready for action. Sleep.

Pete walked into the office and closed the door behind him.

– Ah, said the deskgirl, Mr Lynd wants to see you, Mr Cox.

– Me?

– Who else?

Fair gurgling heads dipped.

– Now?

The girl nodded and tilted her head. Pete marched across to the far door and knocked.

– Come in.

Pete entered.

– Ah.

– I heard you wanted to see me, Mr Lynd.

– Ah yes, I did, said Mr Lynd, palming the lid of a cigarbox. Do come in, will you? Close the door. That's right. Now. Yes. Do sit down, Mr Cox.

– Thank you.

Pete sat down.

– Well now, Mr Cox.

Mr Lynd tapped the desktop.

– Will you smoke? he advanced, his hand straying about the desk.

– No thank you, Mr Lynd.

– Well now, Mr Cox, said Mr Lynd, how are you getting on?

– Oh, said Pete, not so bad you know, Mr Lynd.

Clasping the fingers of both hands and sniffing discreetly, Mr Lynd, his mouth closed, smiled.

– Good, he smiled. And how are you getting on with your work?

– Well, said Pete, I don't think I can supply an answer to that, Mr Lynd. The answer, I should say, would depend upon whether you were finding it satisfactory.

Swivelling on his seat, Mr Lynd glanced at his reflection in the dark glass cabinet.

– Not quite what I meant, he said. But I can tell you, Mr Cox, that your work is, yes, quite satisfactory.

63

- Oh, said Pete, thank you.
- I meant rather, said Mr Lynd, swivelling back on his seat and hitching his trousers, I meant rather, how do you, yourself, feel about it?
- How do I feel about it?
- To be quite frank, Mr Cox, said Mr Lynd, clasping his fist at his belly, some of my colleagues and myself differ.
- Differ?
- I mean in our attitudes towards the workpeople, I mean the staff. Personally, I regard their, er, mental welfare, if you like, as something affecting the efficiency of the firm as a whole.
- Very true, Pete said.
- I tell you this, of course, because I realize, you are not, ah, of course, unintelligent, Mr Cox.

Pete scratched his nose and murmured.

- But what I meant to say, Mr Cox, continued Mr Lynd, his trunk falling forward and his forehead denting, was that I had gathered, um, the impression, once or twice, that you were inclined to be, how shall I put it –

He opened a black leather diary which lay to his right hand on the desk, and shut it firmly.

- – far away.
- Really? Pete said, crossing his right leg over his left.
- Yes, said Mr Lynd, propping his elbows and juggling his fingers, that you weren't keen, shall I say, was my impression, on your work.
- Keen on my work?
- Ah yes, said Mr Lynd, nodding briskly, as it were.

  What do you mean, as it were? Don't give me the needle.
- But I assure you, Mr Lynd, said Pete, I find my work very interesting. I should say concentration has many misleading appearances.

  Watch yourself.
- I beg your pardon? said Mr Lynd, his eyes flattening.
- No, I mean . . .

Mr Lynd grinned frankly, his palms upthrust.

– I didn't quite . . .

– No – Pete began, I –

His foot thumped the desk.

– No, he said, smiling, I'm quite at home, Mr Lynd, if that's what you mean. Probably doing a bit of thinking about the job in hand at those times.

Mr Lynd's forehead snapped up.

– Ah, he said, I'm glad to hear it, Mr Cox. I believe, you see, that you have a great deal of capability.

He sniffed strongly and felt for his pocketwatch.

Who told you that? Your wet nurse? You don't want to believe a word they say, mate. Come on. Dismiss me. Enough. We're like the misses cheese and cream. Admit it. I'm a closed book.

Mr Lynd clacked his pocketwatch shut.

– Tell me, Mr Cox.

– Yes?

– What exactly, if you don't, as it were, he laughed, mind my asking, is your ambition?

Pete watched Mr Lynd open the cigarbox, close it and look up candidly.

– I'm afraid, he replied, stroking his chin, I can't say that I've ever really considered it, Mr Lynd.

– Really? That surprises me.

Mr Lynd blinked, and dug his chin, straightening, to release his neck.

– Because I believe, he said, swallowing, and I am not alone in this, that you have some degree of potentiality where this firm is concerned, to be quite frank.

The sun rubbed upon his arm, as he stretched to push a calendar to the deskedge. He prevented its fall, straddled it to stand, and jolted upright in his chair.

– Yes. But you have, I take it, other interests?

– Oh yes, said Pete, I have a considerable amount of other interests. Domestic mostly.

– Oh? I don't believe you're married?

Mr Lynd's eyes twinkled. Their chuckles joined.

– No, I'm not, Mr Lynd.

– I see. Well, perhaps I'm being a little too inquisitive.

– Not at all.

Mr Lynd lifted his jacketcuff and inspected and flicked at, with his little finger, his shirtcuff.

– Well, he concluded, any time you'd like to speak to me, please don't hesitate to do so.

– That's very kind of you, Mr Lynd.

– Good, said Mr Lynd, resting in his chair.

Pete stood up. The sun splintered the paperweight.

– Thank you, he said.

– No, no.

> Little lamb, who made thee?

The door, closing, furred on the carpet, behind him.

Later in the afternoon, the sun lowering on the city, Pete leaned on the wall at the foot of the stone flight, smoking, watching through the window red buses move under trees by the river.

> No alarm on the river. No sweat on the river. Steel only. Odour of steel. Steel glint on the tide. Armies of light on the metal water. Voices.

Above him, voices. They played light, elusive, descending; dissolved into laughter, high-circling, lower; dwindled to a stone murmur. Shoes scraped and stopped, whispering, above him. Trapped under the stairslope, he, frowning, whispers; they, girls, above the stairhead, urged softly on, laughing, murmuring. Edging, a clicked shoe, metaltipped, sounded down upon stone, clicking unseen on the downward stone, turned, halted. A sigh between voices, low, a juggled cackle. Back against the wallface, Pete heard quick warring whispers, rubbing murmurs wrapped in the stone. One voice now, slid down undeciphered, sliding into the crannied ear, trod on a filament in the grained wall, parcelled, down under echo; its own sound. One voice, leaning, shoes grating a step, stoneslapping, above him, in a husk and pace, heard, unheard; one ceasing, allowing, listening. Pete leaned on the murmured wall, turned his face to the lightglut, listened, allowed. Steps skidded down upon stone, rang the laughter, loud, open, wordless. A door banged.

> Gone. Sweetness. Light. Things rank. Things gross. The kingdom.

He climbed the stairs and entered the office.

– Oh Mr Cox, there's someone on the phone for you.

– What, now?

– Yes. Just rung.

All ears open. Eyes.

– Hullo?

– Mr Cox?

– Yes. Who's that?

– I've phoned up to say that my client is not satisfied with your work on the ceiling.

– What?

– Don't forget you gave my client a guarantee. He's willing to take sixty percent for the castoffs but he can't stand drips. You fulfil your obligations and he'll do the same with his. My client's willing to give you –

– Len, not now, I'm busy. When shall I see you?

– You don't seem to understand the gravity of this situation, Mr Pox, I mean Cox. The plumbing's out of order and the meter's clogging up. The grand piano's probably beyond repair. If you make a bargain it's up to you to keep it. My client –

– Righty-o then. If you're near here, meet me after work.

– This is unheard of.

– Cheerio.

– Don't forget to bring the sauerkraut.

Ten

– I'm here, Len said, wiping his feet on the hallmat. It's not raining.

He unhooked the hallmirror from the wall and carried it down the stairs.

– Put it back, Mark said, following him into the room.

– This is the best piece of furniture you've got in the house. Did you know that? It's Spanish. No, Portuguese. You're Portuguese, aren't you?

– Put it back.

Len screwed his nose and stared.

– I don't understand you, he said.

– Put it back.

– Look in this mirror. Look at your face in this mirror. Look! It's a farce. Your liver's wrapped up in your kidneys. Where are your features? You haven't got any features. You've got a nose here, an ear there. You've been deceiving yourself for years. What's this supposed to be, a face? You look ready for Broadmoor. I don't know why I associate with you.

– Take that mirror back, Len.

– I saw Pete today. I met him after work. You didn't know that. This mirror? What have you got against it? What's the matter with it? I think I'll have to call in your male nurse.

He walked up the stairs and hooked the mirror back on the wall. Mark sat down in an armchair and watched him return and pause in the doorway.

– I wonder about you. I often wonder about you, Len murmured. But I must keep pedalling. I must. There's a time limit.

– Is there?

– Yes.

He smiled and looked about the room.

– Who have you got hiding here? What? You're not alone here.

– You're quite right.

– Hmn. How are you getting on with your Esperanto? Don't forget, anything over two ounces goes up a penny.

– Thanks for the tip, Mark said.

– Yes, but what tips can you give me? None. I'll go. I'm rusty. I can't do it. What do you care? You don't know. But I'll tell you. Do you know where I've just been?

– No.

– I've been to the Conway Hall. I've just heard the Grosse Fuge. I've never heard anything like it. It's not musical. It's physical. It's physical. It's not music. It's someone sawing bones in a coffin.

– Really?

– I saw Pete today.

– You said.

– I met him after work. We walked along the Embankment. He asked me to lend him a quid.

– Well?

– I refused.

– What?

– You don't understand. I told him if I lent him a quid it would be an event. And I don't want anything to do with events.

Mark closed one eye and squinted, lighting a cigarette.

– What did he say to that? he asked.

– What did he say? He said. He spoke. He had his say. Do you know something? Since I left him I've been thinking thoughts I've never thought before. I've been thinking thoughts I've never thought before.

He waved his arms and dropped them.

– Look here, Mark said.

– What?

- Why don't you leave Pete alone?
- Leave him alone?
- Why don't you give it a rest? He doesn't do you any good.
- What did you say?
- I'm the only one who can get on with him, Mark said.
- You?
- Yes. You've got to have a certain kind of – something – to get on with him. Anyway, I've got it and at the moment you haven't. What good does he do you? You should give it a rest.
- You get on with him? Len said.
- He doesn't take any liberties with me. He does with you.
- What makes you think he takes liberties with me?
- Do what you bloodywell like.
- You mean come over to your side.
- What do you mean? Mark said.

Len unhooked the toastingfork from the wall and peered at it.

- This is a work of genius.
- What did you mean by that?
- Do you ever make any toast?

The fork slipped from Len's hand as he turned it to the light and dropped on to the carpet. Mark bent forward.

- Don't touch it! Len hissed, cutting the air with his hands. No! You don't know what will happen if you touch it. Jesus Christ'll come up if you touch it. Don't you know that? You're frightened of Christ, aren't you? He frightens you.
- Do me a favour, will you?
- No, but he makes you shiver, doesn't he?

Len bent swiftly and lifted the fork from the floor.

- There you are. Nothing happens when I touch it. No one would bother. I'm in a musty old clothescupboard. I stink of old clothes. I'm only fit for the boiler room. You can see that. Tar, sweat, engines. That's all. Do you know how you're looking at me? Excuse me if I laugh. I'll laugh tomorrow. You're looking at me as if I were a human being. You're an old hand at this game, I know, but it's no use looking at me like that. You're trying to look me straight in the eye and I'm looking at your navel. Or are you looking down my throat? If you are, I'm sure you can see a long way down. Anyway, I prefer to stare glasseyed at the navel. When I can. What else do you want me to do? What else can I do? I was never one to prescribe remedies. What about you? I'm sure your remedy would cause a lot of good clean shitting all over the place. So would Pete's. But they're not my remedies. I don't prescribe remedies.

He dropped into an armchair, clutching the toastingfork, and slowly let it slide to his side, covering his eyes.

– You see – I can't see the broken glass. I can't see the mirror I have to look through. I see the other side. The other side. But I can't see the mirror side.

His head lolling, he keened.

– I want to break it, all of it. But how can I break it? How can I break it when I can't see it?

He hissed through his teeth and shook his head fiercely.

– You're stone. Am I dead in you? I've shot the bolt. If I could move from this chair I'd go.

– Pete and Virginia will be round any minute, Mark said.

– That's all right. That, I tell you, is all right! Leave me alone. What do you want? Ah. Sniff this room. Sniff it. This room has changed since I've been in it. I've permeated it. It's all acrid now.

– You're wrong. The room's the same.

– No. Don't give me that. You don't know. You've no idea what a jackal you've got in this room.

– Yes I have.

– No. You think you know something about me but you don't. Do you know what I am? I'm the ragamuffin who vomits in the palace. There's a dryrot in me. Rot everywhere. What about the worm that ate a building down? That's what it's like. I could stay in this armchair for ever. Or in bed. Yes. Do you know, I can't step out of bed? I'm unable to step out of the bed. I can't put my foot on the floor. I could stay there, always. Have people come and feed me. They could do that easily enough. Yes, you don't know. You don't know what you've got in this room. A sack of old bones. But can't you understand? I can't even commit suicide. It's got to be a decision. That's an action. I can't act. I'm not justified in committing suicide. It would be worthless, meaningless. Suicide isn't meaningless. It's an action. That's what it is.

II

Eleven

What are the dwarfs doing, in their journeys to the street-corners? They stumble in the gutters and produce their pocket-watches. One with a face of chalk chucks the dregs of the day into a bin and seats himself on the lid. He is beginning to chew though he has not eaten. Now they collect at the backstep. One scrubs his veins at the lower sink, now he is gorged in the sud. Spruced and preened, in time for the tuck. Time is kept to the T.

Pete is in the cabin. He cannot hear the backchat of bone from the yard, the crosstalk of bristled skin. He is listening to himself. Now Mark, who combs his hair in mirrors. He holds six pocket-mirrors at related angles. He sings the song of Mark to the cocked glass. He does not see the market outside the window. He sees himself and smiles.

The floor is scrubbed to the grain, my own work.

It is to this fund I donate, and sublet the premises. I strike a shrewd bargain. I am the promoter, although neither Pete nor Mark is aware of the contract, nor of the contractor.

They are still there, the two of them. Or perhaps they have gone. We must wait. I am prepared to wait. I do not want to stop waiting. The end of this vigil is the beginning of nothing.

Twelve

- Come away, come away, death, and in sad cypress let me be laid, Pete sang.

The sun was setting. Lilac hung heavy on the arched tree. The garden flickered. In low deckchairs Len and Mark were lying. Pete gravely ended the dirge, standing at the garden door.

- I like this garden. It's tranquil.

In a lower garden a bonfire, burning, collapsed, in a gash, splintered. Smoke smarted thinly across the fences.

- My mind's a blank, Mark said.
- Say the first thing, Len said, that comes into it.
- Shaving in the asylum of Wednesday I saw a toadstool sitting on a blank rabbit, Mark said in one breath.
- Blimey!
- There you are.
- I'll tell you what, Pete said, thinking got me into this and thinking's got to get me out. You know what I want? An efficient idea. Do you know what I mean? An efficient idea. One that'll work. Something I can pin my money on. An eachway bet. Nothing's guaranteed, I know that. But I'm willing to gamble. I've never stopped gambling but I'm a bit cramped these days. That's what I need. Do you know what I mean? Of course, some people are efficient ideas in themselves. You might be an efficient idea yourself, Mark. You can never tell. I wouldn't like to pass judgement. But I'm not. I've got to sweat for one. And if I can get hold of one I've got to make it a going concern. No grafting and no fiddling. Some people can afford to take three or four days off a week. I can't afford the time. Do you know what I mean?
- I should think they're very few and far between, efficient ideas, Mark said.

- They may be. But I told you, thinking got me into this and thinking's got to get me out.
- I once knew a man who didn't think, Mark said. He rushed home as fast as he could every evening, turned the armchair round, sat in it and looked out of the window. After about two hours, when it was dark, he'd get up and turn on the light.
- Yes, Len said, but I know what you mean about an efficient idea. Like a nutcracker. You press the cracker and the cracker cracks the nut. There's no waste of energy. It's an exact process and an efficient one. The idea's efficient.
- No, Pete said, you're wrong. There is waste. When you press the cracker with the proper purchase the nut cracks, but at the same time the hinge of the cracker gives out a friction, a heat, which is incidental. It's unnecessary to the particular idea. It's nearly efficient but not quite. Because there's an escape and wastage of energy to no purpose. It's uneconomic. It's exactly the same, after all, with a work of art. Every particle of a work of art should crack a nut, or help form a pressure that'll crack the final nut. Do you know what I mean? Each idea must possess stringency and economy and the image, if you like, that expresses it must stand in exact correspondence and relation to the idea. Only then can you speak of utterance and only then can you speak of achievement. If there's any excess heat or friction, if there's any waste, you've failed and you have to start again. It's simple enough.
- But what about the sun and moon? Len said. Isn't there something ambiguous about the sun and moon?
- Then again, Pete went on, there's nothing against a geezer constructing his own efficient idea, but he's got to be quite sure, in the first place, what he means by the term efficient. And once he's understood it, he's got to determine to what the idea is relevant, or whether it's relevant at all. Some ideas that were adequate enough in the past wouldn't take you farther than the Edgware Road now. You've got to be

able to distinguish between a workaday efficiency and a relative one, one that might have been relevant once, or might be relevant in different circumstances, but isn't now. It's a matter of considering what world you're relating it to.

– Well, we can't make any mistake about that, said Mark.

– I don't know, Pete said. I don't know that we quite agree on that point, Mark.

– You mean we may be talking about two different things?

– Yes. What it comes down to is what world, exactly, are you talking about?

– What world? The whole gamut as far as you can sniff. Backwards and forward and in and out.

– Yes, but I sometimes think you're omitting to sniff relevant matters which are right under your nose. You know what I mean?

– I think I sniff what you're getting at all right.

– Well, quite frankly, Mark, I suggest you don't pay enough attention to what goes on around you.

– You mean the headlines.

– There's more to it than that. You're subject to what goes on around you and you depend on it for your welfare and existence. I don't see how you can fail to be involved. This is the society you live in and I wouldn't say you're fulfilling your part of the bargain.

– You refer to the busticket world.

– All right. You have tuppence in your pocket and you pay your fare. But it seems to me you regard that tuppence, and more to the point, the conveyance itself, as a divine right. The way you pay your tuppence you don't really pay it at all. You're getting a free ride. You don't fully realize that the tuppence is sweat and the ride is sweat too.

– I'm a liability on the world's bank balance.

– You're not only a liability, Pete laughed, you're a bloody hallucination! Sometimes I can't believe you exist at all.

– But where you do believe I exist, Mark said, is as a parasite.

– Not entirely.

78

- A parasite, Mark said, standing up. But it's inaccurate. I don't live on anyone's earnings. I don't pinch anything from the till. I've nothing but contempt for the till. I'm not concerned with the standards you're talking about. I follow my itch, that's all. It's not going up your alley, it may not be going up anyone's alley, so what? I don't aspire to the great standards. They don't apply to me. I don't live with them.
- That's the point, Pete said. What I'm accusing you of is operating on life and not in it.
- If I'm a ponce, Mark said, I'm my own ponce. I'm nobody else's ponce. I live and I operate in my own life.
- You can't live safely tucked up in a test tube.
- You're off the beam.
- Your danger, Mark, is that you might become nothing but an attitude.
- Not while I've still got balls, mate.
- They won't save you. They might drop off.
- I keep them well oiled.
- Look. What I'm objecting to is that you tend to take a bit of a holiday in between times.
- If I do, they're not with pay. I fork out. Anyway the term holiday isn't valid. You use the term holiday because I'm deviating from your course. I'm not deviating from my own.
- Ah, Pete said, there may be some truth in that. I told you, you might be an efficient idea.

He passed Mark a cigarette and struck a match.

- What you don't understand about me, Mark said, is this – I've got no ambition.

Pete looked at him.

- Oh, he said. I see.
- Listen, Mark snapped. It's about time I told you people something else – for your own good.
- What?
- Did you know I was born circumcised?
- What!

- The geezer came along with the carvingknife to do the necessary and nearly dropped down dead with the shock. They had to give him a doublebrandy on the house. He thought I was the Messiah.
- Well, Len asked, own up. Are you?

Later, they left the house and walked past the pond to the Swan café, to meet Virginia. She had arrived, and was sitting in the corner.

- Well, Pete said, as they sat down with tea, how's Marie?
- She's very well, said Virginia.
- Marie Saxon? said Mark. What's she doing now?
- She spends most of her time, Pete said, in Soho. Prancing about with all and sundry.
- Is she still in love with me?
- She didn't mention it, Virginia said.
- She was mad about me, Mark said, in the old days.
- She isn't the one, Pete asked, that you banged round the earhole once?
- No. That was Rita.
- Oh yes. Rita.
- What was that? Len asked.
- She was leading him up the garden, Pete laughed, or something, so he knocked her teeth in.
- Not quite, Mark said, but she asked for it, anyway. It was the biggest surprise of her life. I've got no regrets. Taught her respect. Listen Len. Don't look at me like that. You didn't know the girl. There was room for no other action, I assure you. So Marie's not in love with me, any more, eh?
- Love? Pete said. She's flogging her whatsit to bellboys and pisshounds.

From the inner room of the café came the sound of a guitar, strummed heavily.

- What have you all been doing? asked Virginia.
- Chatting, Pete said. A social evening.
- Right, said Mark.

- I was trying to explain to Len, Pete said, how he'd benefit under my health scheme, but he wouldn't listen.
- What's the book, Virginia? Mark asked.
- *Hamlet*.
- *Hamlet?* Pete said.
- What's it like?
- Do you know, Virginia said, it's odd, but I suddenly can't find any virtue in the man.
- Really? Mark said.
- No.
- Why?
- No, she said, no, I – after all, what is he? What is he but vicious, maudlin, spiteful, and sensitive to nothing but his own headaches? I find him completely unprepossessing.

She sat back, tapping her spoon on the table. A voice was raised, from the inner room, singing in Italian to the guitar.

- Well, Mark laughed, it's a point of view.
- You're quite wrong, Pete said, of course.
- I don't know, Virginia murmured. What does he do but talk and talk, and now and again stick a knife into someone. I mean a sword.
- I find this rather amusing, Pete said. But we won't go into it.
- I've got to go, Len said, standing up.
- Yes, Pete said, we'll adjourn.
- Allnight shift? Mark asked, as they walked to the door.
- Yes, Len said. There's my bus.
- Be seeing you, said Pete.

Len ran across the road.

- You can see yourself home, Ginny? Pete said. I think I'll go straight back.
- Of course.
- Shall I see you home? Mark said.
- No, no, it's quite all right.
- My bus, Pete said. See you. Ta-ta, Mark.

He walked across the road.

– Well, Virginia said, I'd better be off.
Mark watched her lips move.
– I can easily –
– No, it's all right, Mark. It's only five minutes.
– How are you? he asked.
– Fine.
– Uh-huh.
– Well, she said, I'd better be going. I'll be seeing you.
– Yes.
– Cheerio.
– Goodnight, Mark said.
– Goodnight.

Thirteen

Pete walked quickly out of the office and across the road. He found an empty telephone box and went into it. While the bell rang he looked into the street.

- Ginny?
- Yes.
- Are you in?
- In? Of course.
- All right. I'm coming round now.
- What's the hurry?
- I'll be there in half an hour.
- Is anything wrong?
- Don't go out.

He caught a bus to Dalston. At the trafficlights he jumped off and took a short cut behind the station. Virginia opened the door of her flat in her bathrobe.

- You were very quick. I've just had a bath.
- What for? Pete asked.
- What?

He went into the kitchen, took off his jacket and tie and washed his face at the sink.

- Did you have a bad day?

Seizing the towel, he turned.

- What do you mean, bad day?
- Bad day. Bad day.
- Why have you had a bath?
- It's hot.

He threw the towel aside, returned to the living room, sat down in an armchair, lit a cigarette, blew the match, and looked up to see Virginia, her bathrobe open, regarding her body.

- Look how pink my nipples are. Like a virgin, she said.
- Will you do that thing up?
- Why?
- Do you mind doing it up?

She tied the cord and sat at the table. From her handbag she took a cigarette and lit it.

- Who was round here this afternoon?
- How do you know anyone was here?
- The cups, the cups. Who was it?
- My friend Marie Saxon.
- What did she want?
- A cup of tea.
- What did she want?
- Christ. She didn't want anything.
- She's a prostitute.
- No she's not.
- She's a scrubber.

A breeze blew the curtains. Virginia smoothed her hair.

- Did you have your bath while she was here?
- Why?
- Did she soap your armpits?

Pete looked about the room.

- Where are the drawingpins I left here, and the draw-
  ingboard?
- Here. Somewhere.
- Where?
- They're not down the bloody drain.
- If you become involved with Marie Saxon, Virginia, that's
  where you'll end up.
- Christ.
- Will you stop saying that?
- No, I don't know what to say.
- Why say anything?
- Ah.
- And for God's sake, he shouted, keep that robe done up! I
  don't want to see the hair on your crutch. What do you

think I am?

She stood up, closed her robe and sat again.

– I don't know what I think you are.

– I know you don't. I'm damn sure you don't. It's about time you stopped continually powdering your fanny and opened your eyes, mate. Why, for instance, don't you go and put some clothes on now? You've made your point. It only needs a little effort to get out of this masturbatory rut.

– What are you talking about?

– Don't you realize, he said, that someone might knock on that door and that you've no right to open it like that?

– You could open it.

– You're being very disappointing, Virginia. You know what you're doing, don't you? You're behaving like any other little tart who must show herself off or cease to exist.

– I've just had a bath.

– It's normal to dress after a bath.

– Oh for God's sake!

Pete threw his cigarette into the grate.

– So, he said, if there's a knock on the door, you'll go to it like that?

– I don't expect anyone.

– Don't be stupid. Anyone's liable to turn up. A man may come to examine the meters.

– He only comes in the mornings.

– How can you be sure?

– He's at home, Virginia said, mowing the garden.

She began to chew a crumb, and then rose and went to the sideboard, where she picked up a copy of *Picture Post* and flicked the pages.

– If you could start to think, Virginia, you might be a little more use to me. As it is, quite honestly, you're nothing but a dead weight. I know there are men who would be glad to accept you as you are, but I needn't enlarge upon them. We know their requirements. Of course, it may be that their requirements are yours too. It's quite possible that I've been suffering under a delusion about you. If that is the case, why don't you get Marie Saxon to introduce you to some motorcyclists, or all-in wrestlers?

– Yes, I'll think about that.
– What else do you think about, Virginia?
– Nothing else.
– I wonder, Pete said, what you and Marie Saxon discuss?
– Only one thing. Jockstraps.
– Yes of course, most women have minds like mouldy larders. It could hardly be otherwise, I suppose. I remember the last time I saw Marie Saxon. She was in a swimming costume. Her breasts were flopping about like washing on a line. She exists within that framework, such as it is, of course. Her life naturally resolves itself into a neverending bout of selftitillation. That's what she understands by life. But if you're falling into that error, I'm disappointed, to be quite frank. I've told you before where your beauty lies. If –
– Pete! What do you want? What do you want? What do you want?

She ran across the room and fell at his knees.

– What do you want me to do? What have I done? Please! What have I done? Tell me. Tell me.

He looked down at her.

– Why did you say that thing about *Hamlet* last night?
– What thing?
– About *Hamlet*. Why did you say it? Why do you say these things? Do you know they're extremely stupid? It made me look very foolish. Did you realize that? You don't know anything about *Hamlet*, Ginny. Don't you understand that? And yet you come in with the book under your arm. Why did you do that, in the first place? Was it to make an impression? Are you mad? Did you think Mark would be impressed? If so, at what? Mark was amused. But I wasn't. It's up to you entirely – in point of fact it's a matter of distinct choice – a choice you'll have to make – but the point is, Ginny, that while we're together I can't have you making

such ridiculous statements about something you know nothing about. It's out of all proportion. You made me look, in effect, a bloody fool. I thought I told you to leave Shakespeare for a while? Don't you think it was for your own good? I've told you you're nowhere near the point where you can begin to absorb his implications, and not only do you ignore what I say but you lug the book about with you like a pissy fifthformer, and parade these stupidities. It's quite absurd but it's more than absurd. It's pathetic. And not only is it pathetic but it's bloody niggling. I've told you to leave him alone, I've told you you're not capable of expressing an opinion about him, which isn't a reflection on you, because not two out of a hundred are capable, I've told you of the study you've got to do, I've surely given you an inkling as to the complexity of the whole question, I've even asked you to reach a position of being able to inform me, through study, so I must have had some respect for your powers, and this is how you act. Do you realize that that statement was an abortion? Where did you read it? Wherever you read it you didn't even digest the idea. Could you have argued upon that statement, with reference to the text? Of course not. Did you think such palpable emotionalism would pass as critical comment? In other less charitable company you would have had your balls chopped off. You were really very fortunate no word was said. I decided not to, then. You had showed both of us up enough, as it was. What must Mark and Len think? I'm supposed to have some concern for your literary development and suddenly, under my auspices, as it were, you come out with that. But what, I want to know, was your motive? What did you hope to prove? That you could form your own opinions? To prove to Mark that you could read? Do you think that if you carried a book on Advanced Mathematics under your arm you would necessarily persuade Len you could add two and two? You didn't seriously imagine you were presenting a brand new idea? Don't you realize that that idea, though not your crummy expression of it, has been chewed over and gobbed up from start to finish, and mostly by incompetents? Don't you realize that it is in itself incompetent, superficial and gauche? But it's not worth talking about. What I don't understand is your motive. Were you deliberately trying to make me look a fool? No, it was probably just – here I am, listen to me – but you forget you weren't in your school commonroom, Virginia. God knows what you say there that probably passes for God's word. It's lamentable. Now look here, you're bound to think of what you say before you say it and you're obliged, this is the point, to realize, once and for all, your limitations. You're morally obliged. That was nothing but an unforgivable error of judgement, as applied to time, place and content. You seem to have no sense of fitness or context. So far from doing any good you did positive harm. It was morally indefensible and morally objectionable. Because from what did it spring? A desire to assert. It was pure bloody bombast, illconsidered, faulty, inept, preposterous and shaming, and what's more, entirely unpolitic. Did you think we were all going to bow down at your altar? Did you think you would be excused because you were a woman? Well, whatever you thought, Virginia, quite honestly it's not very satisfactory. I find it all very dubious. I put a considerable degree of faith in you, I damnwell do my best to educate you, and all you do is make a fool of both of us. Now listen here, what I want you to understand is this. In other societies you're entitled to do what you like, but while we're together, I refuse to put up with this kind of behaviour. It's for your own good as well as mine. I'm willing to help you all I can in such matters, but such an action on your part almost amounts to a stab in the back. Now it's no use saying you won't repeat this sort of thing if you're still going to feel the inclination. What you must do is develop a sense of proportion, of judgement. You have the faculties but you seem reluctant to use them. Why are you crying? I tell you, you have the faculties. It's just a matter of bringing them into focus, of sharpening them. I've always admired them in you. You've no need to cry. I know you've understood me. All that happened was that your artistic sensibility, your sense of proportion, went astray. I'm quite sure, in fact, that you realize that, Ginny. I admire these qualities in you, I always have done, I merely felt bound to point out –

– I'm sorry, Virginia said, her head in her hands, I'm sorry. I won't do it again.
– No, Pete said, rising, sitting on the chairarm, and holding her to his chest, it's all right. It's all right.
– I'm sorry, Virginia said, I'm sorry.
– No, Pete said, it's all right. It's all right.

Fourteen

- Why don't you put it on the table? What's up your nose now?
- What do you want me to say?
- Open it up, Len. I can't see you for the cobwebs.
- You must excuse me. I'm in the centre of a holy plague.
- Do you want me to send out a cart to bury the dead?
- Are you a nonprofitmaking concern?
- Of course I'm not, Mark said. Who is? What are you saying?
- Sometimes you're a snake, to me, Len hissed.
- Now don't get me against the ropes, Len.
- You're a snake in my house.
- Really?
- It's a question of motive. I don't trust your motives, Mark. I can understand you're after some profit from all comers. Yes, who isn't. But I smell a rat when it seems you're trying to buy and sell my firm. It's the action of a snake. What do you think I am, a ventriloquist's dummy? I object to opening my mouth and saying something you've put into it. By insinuation. That happens. As for you, you sit and watch points. You weigh me. You keep a tab on me. You cash in all the time. How much are you making? You think you're on to a good thing. I could even accuse you of working out my casehistory, though I have no substantial evidence. Quite honestly I wouldn't put it past you. But I object very strongly to this buying and selling of me, this sticking labels on my every word, my every action. You've got the scientific mind, not Pete. That's what the world doesn't appreciate. Am I wronging you? All right, how calculated is it? It appears to me quite often, Mark, very calculated. I don't like the smell. I don't want to see through

your eyes or anybody's eyes. I have enough trouble making ends meet as it is. What are you after? I tell you I won't have a snake in my house.

Mark stood up, walked into the kitchen and poured himself a glass of water. He drank it and stood in the doorway.

– Balls, he said.

– That doesn't mean a thing to me.

– What are you waiting for, a statement for the defence?

– That's up to you.

– Aaah! Mark grated.

He sat down on the edge of a chair, coughed shortly and spat in the fireplace.

– Still, I'm glad you've said all this, he said, belching and wiping his mouth. Who knows? You may be right. Your conclusion is I'm a snooper? Why should I answer?

– You want me to leave your house?

– Do what you like.

Len clenched his fist and thumped the chairarm.

– So you've got nothing to say?

– No.

– Do you understand what I was talking about?

– Yes.

– And you don't agree?

Mark shrugged.

– You disagree?

Mark cleared his throat and hawked. He banged his chest and spat.

– What?

– You think I'm mistaken?

Mark shrugged.

– But am I? Apart from what I think and you think, am I?

– Am you?

– Am I?

Mark shrugged and sniffed. He blew his nose.

– What's the matter with you tonight? Len said. You're farting and belching all over the place.

91

– Uh.

– Aaah! Len rasped, and rattled his head, shivering. Do you or do you not stick labels on me?

– Not as far as I know.

– Are you telling the truth?

Mark eased back in the chair and crossed his legs.

– Of course, Len said, you may not know the truth yourself. Yes, yes, that's quite possible. That's a possibility. I'm just unable to wind this thread up. It's eating me away.

He raked his hair.

– You're too big for me, he murmured. You and Pete, you're too big. You leave me dry. You eat me out of house and home, whether you damnwell know it or not. I sometimes feel I'm the ball you're both playing with.

– Why should you be?

– Sometimes I'm all right. And then the room becomes full of ice. I don't understand. I don't understand Pete, but I can feel him at a distance, sometimes. You I can seldom feel at a distance and I don't understand you either. You're not as simple as you look. But I know one thing. You've made a deeper hole in my side than I thought at first. Yes. I suppose there's a lot to be said for feeling the world at a distance. I have known it. But mostly the world is sitting on top of me. Maybe it's really at a distance then. Who knows? Maybe there's no such thing as distance. But we know there is!

He smacked his forehead.

– I've lost a kingdom.

Mark picked up the toastingfork and held it behind his ear.

– I respond, you see, Len said, only to the intimate and minute. I prefer it that way. If only I could close my eyes and live alone with suggestions of life. I can't live comfortably when the world begins to bang. And at work I don't lift a finger. I don't even kick anyone. But it's very clearcut there. A train comes in, people get out, everyone knows what to do. Someone drops dead on the platform and everyone knows what to do. It's easy. And it is easy. I don't deny it. What could be easier? I suppose you're taking good care of things. Did you know that you and Pete are a musichall act? I know nothing about Pete, except that his world sets every day and he has to resurrect it forcibly. I have an inkling of that. But the two of them. Him and Ginny. What happens? I think when they're alone they must do a jig, a dance, that nobody else could understand. What happens? But I know nothing of these things. It's a closed book and it's too big for me. But is it big? I must be able to tell the big from the small. If I can't do that I might as well cut the cable. I suppose you're taking good care of things. For me, you see, I don't grow old. I change. I don't die. I change again. I am not happy. I change. Nor unhappy. But when a big storm takes place I do not change. I become someone else, which means I change out of all recognition. I am transformed from the world in which I suffer the changes I suffer, I retreat utterly from the standpoint where I am subject to change, then with my iron mask on, in a guise of which I understand nothing, less than before, I wait for the storm to pass. But at the same time it is, I admit, impossible for me in these moments to sit quite still without wanting to go back. It's also impossible in these moments not to feel the itch to go forward. I must learn restraint. Anyway, I suppose you're taking good care of things. Just because you've put a penny in my slot you think I'll go on talking for ever. But you're wrong. My gas, the gas, is running out. But I'm not casting off till I've made sure of my provisions for a long journey. I know what it's like to be caught short, unprepared, unprotected because of lack of forethought. It may be I shall spend all my time collecting provisions and never cast off from the shore. I'm fed up with talking but I shall always talk. Maybe that's my business. Everyone has his or her job. But I can only get the window half open. The window refuses to open.

He took off his glasses and placed them in his lap.

– But I can tell you one thing. Mysteries are always new mysteries, I've decided that. So, you see, I am alive and not a storehouse of dead advice and formulas of how to live. And I won't be. But I have to be silent, like the guilty.

He looked up and put on his glasses.

– Did you know that the suspicious and the dead have one thing in common? They are silent. Of course, I put my suspicions on the table tonight and I wasn't silent. So you think I'm contradicting myself, but if you think that I'm prepared to go further. Actually, and you can take it or leave it, I am neither suspicious nor dead. I am not. Weinstein may be. The trouble, the real trouble, is, though, that I cannot convince myself that I'm not spiritually dead. Quite frankly, the evidence is overwhelming, if to be dead in such a way means the ability only to communicate with the past, the inability to communicate with the present. I sometimes communicate with you, occasionally with Pete.

– Pete? Mark said. The only real communication for you with him would be surrender. He'd consume. He'd be the one, mate, that would eat you out of house and home. I've told you, it's about time you did yourself a favour.

– You're wrong and right.

Mark frowned. He moved to the sideboard, picked up an apple and bit into it.

– Yes, Len said, I say I communicate sometimes. But whether I do or not doesn't matter. I do just the same.

– Yes?

– It's a corner, you see, I occupy a corner. I am unable to speak to anyone, most of the time, without there being a complexity which repels me. I am unable to consider myself without finding myself repellent.

– Are you at a dead end?

– You mean have I no potential? Yes, I have potential, certainly. Do you know what it's like? It's like the useless buried Spanish treasure galleons. It will not come to the surface, ever. All my days, Mark, are lived with a sight of my own buried treasure. It's in my corner, somewhere. Everything is in my corner. All I said to you earlier is contained there. Everything is from the corner's point of view. I don't hold the whip. I'm a labouring man. I do the corner's will. I slave my guts out, and get nothing out of it. I thought, at one time, that I'd escaped it, but it never dies, it's never dead. So I can never hope to see things as they are, or might really be. Of course, I can understand that my corner is the whole too. I feed it. It's well fed. Things that at one time seem to me of value I have no resource but to give it to eat and what was of value turns into pus. I can hide nothing. I can't lay anything aside.

He leaned forward in the chair.

– Look, I'm finished with buried treasure. Mine is here now, instant and ready. Why don't you take it? You have it. I give it to you. Take it.

– No thanks. You can keep it.

– Listen, Len said. I know the corner is a necessary, an evident particle of living, a whole within a whole, if you like, but I know I know I've got to die in some way to get out of it. Something has to die. I may be emerging. I'm not dead in it, at all events. You could say I was dead and alive at successive times. In, out. In, out, dead, alive. Some people would call it an interesting period.

They stared at each other. Mark slapped his head.

– I'll have to use a stopwatch in a minute!

– What can I do? Len asked, bending double in the chair, guffawing. What, I ask you, can I do?

Mark walked across the room, thumping his ribs.

– When you say you can't get out you are out!

– Where is out? Len asked, jumping up.

– It's not in, Mark said, retreating into a corner.

– You're not out if you're in, Len said. You're quite right!

– Look at it this way. When you're out you're out, and when you're in you're in.

– I'll write you out a prescription in a minute!

Mark groaned. He went to the table and opened two bottles of beer.

– Listen here, Len said. What I'm really doing, if you want to know the truth, is trying to get my weight down to the limit. Otherwise I lose my purse money and you don't get your 10 per cent.

– I'd give up shadowboxing and go on the road if I were you, Mark said.

– What have you got in here? Len asked, opening the cupboard. Have you got any gherkins? Do you know what I did the other day? I showed a bloke at work, an Oxford student, one of your poems. We'd just met the Irish mail and we both got a five bob tip. So I showed him one of your poems.

– How did he take it? Mark asked.

– He looked at his watch. He said we'd better get across to number seven. The point about these people is, that when they read a poem, they never open the door and go in. They bend down and take a squint through the keyhole. That's all they do.

– They're the intelligent people, Mark said.

– Yes. I've seen their stuff too. It's lucid all right. There's no denying it. But when you feel the quality, there's nothing there. You pick it up like a piece of cloth and you can see right through it. I can't talk to them. How could I tell this bloke that one phrase in your poem wasn't English but Chinese. It's Chinese. That phrase is Chinese. How could I tell him that?

– Which phrase?

– It's not important. I don't remember.

They drank.

– The trouble is, Len said, that I can't follow their terms of reference. I'm a stranger. You see, my reaction to poetry is like the old women eating onions and knitting when the guillotine falls. That's what it is. What do you mean? I don't like the word style. I don't know what it means. I don't like the word style and I don't like the word function.

- These people, said Mark, want everything to fit into their crossword puzzle and they object when a piece doesn't fit, that's all. To hell with them. They've got minds like a backyard bog, mate, even though their shit comes out wrapped in silk and satin.

He picked a buttend from the ashtray and held it up.

- That's what those sort of people are worth.
- I don't know about that.
- What's the good of being shy of contempt? Mark said. Be prepared to condemn and despise, Len. Then the plate's clean.
- I don't believe it.
- Well, how *is* the poetry business? Yours, I mean.
- Finished.
- Bankrupt? Haven't you got any small change in the safe?
- Yes, but it's of no value. I showed that bloke one of my poems too. He hasn't looked at me since. He took it as a personal insult that I should even show it to him. Do you know how I write a poem? I sit in the room and look up at the corners. Suddenly I get up and squeeze a lemon, a drop of juice comes out, and that's the poem. What's the good of that?
- There are no hard and fast rules.
- No?

Mark shifted a curtain and looked out into the night.

- Do you know what these people do? Len said. They climb from word to word, like steppingstones.

He walked about the room, demonstrating.

- Like steppingstones. But tell me this. What do they do when they come to a line with no words in it all? Can you answer that? What do they do when they come to a line with no words in it at all? Can you tell me that?

Mark drained his beer.

- As for you, Len said, I'll tell you what you do when you write a poem. You press button B and get your money back.

97

Fifteen

Virginia sat in an armchair, resting a glass on her lap. With her spoon she poked at the tealeafed lemonstrip and watched the sun move among the vases. The others were talking. She straightened her skirt at her knees, leaned forward to place the glass on the mantelpiece, lay back and closed her eyes.

– Our intellectuals and the masses? Pete was saying. They do one of four things. They either ignore them, pity them, re-create them to mean something else, or complain about them. If you do the first you limit your scope and you're a fool. If you do the second you're not an intellectual. If you do the third you're wasting your time. And if you do the fourth you're just like me.

– What is a mass? Mark asked.

– Get out of it. Haven't you ever heard of the poor, down-trodden, hardpressed, chainganged, pulverized lot of Jesuses who tell us what to do?

– They only go about in hired cars, Len said. I've never seen one of them.

Mark swallowed the remains in his glass.

– Very good tea that, Virginia.

– Good.

– Look here, Len said, I'll tell you something for nothing. I went into the washroom at work the other day and the stationmaster, the big boss, the king of the castle, was bending over a basin washing his hands, immaculately dressed. I couldn't believe my eyes. I stood there looking at him and I had a terrible temptation to kick him straight up the arse.

– Did you? Mark said.

– No. Do you know why? Can't you see why? If I'd have

kicked him there and then and knocked him through the mirror, don't you know what he would have done? He'd have turned round and said, I'm most awfully sorry, wiped his hands, and gone out. Like God. It's exactly what God would do. It stands to reason.

– Yes, Pete said, after a while, it's all very well, but you've got to keep a firm grip on your inclinations in these places. You've got to be armourplated. There's a lot I could do and say if I behaved like a man and lost my temper. But what's the point? I'd rather cut my throat than bandy words with the kind of guttersnipe I run into. Of course, what these people don't understand is that it's not necessary to spy through my cracks. I'm open and above board. Even the devil can peep without temerity.

– Eh? Mark said.

Virginia collected the glasses and took them into the kitchen.

– All right, Pete said, but with my hand on my thumper I'll say this. The art of dealing with others is one, to be able to see through them, and two, to keep your trap shut. If you've got kop enough for the first and control enough for the second you're a made man.

She washed, wiped and set the glasses in the dresser.

– Croquet weather, Len said, it's croquet weather.

– The duke's a long time coming said the duchess, stirring the tea with her other hand, Mark yawned.

– Yes, Pete said, but there's no real weather in London. London doesn't admit to seasons. London's an overall condition. Know what I mean?

Virginia looked out on to the lawn.

– The point is, of course, Pete said, that we weren't born into a world of space at all, but into a nut. The best of us only scrape the sides. Come on, Weinblatt. Do your best and put a frown on. I'm getting on to metaphysics.

Virginia came back into the room and sat down.

– I've discovered an art, Mark said, to find the mind's construction in the arse.

99

- I wouldn't put it past you, said Len.
- No, Pete said, this lavatory culture has its limitations. Being a literary shithouse attendant isn't the sole aim in life. Jesus Christ, for instance, was worth his salt in other directions.
- That's a lovely dress, Virginia, Len said, standing up.
- Haven't you seen it before?
- Have I?
- Pete made it.
- Yes, it's a good fit, that dress, Pete said.
Len bent down and fingered the dress at her shoulder.
- That's a very fair piece of material.
- Wholesale or retail? Mark asked.
- Wholesale. I know a bloke.
- How much are you retail then? Len said.
- I'm not in season, Virginia said.
- Couldn't I get hold of a fair copy in Marks and Spencer's?
- I was lucky with that material, Pete said. I'm working on another garment now.
- What's that? Mark asked.
- A petticoat.
Pete and Mark lit cigarettes, bending to the match from their seats.
- When are you going to do a job of work, Mark?
- Not for sometime yet.
- Where do you get your pocketmoney? Come on. You must be short on your savings by now.
- I've got a duchess in Hanover Square.
- Old or young? asked Virginia.
- She's bedridden.
- I don't doubt it, Pete said.
- As a matter of fact, Mark said, that is my earnest ambition. It's the only way.
- Don't kid yourself. You wouldn't be any good as a gigolo, Pete said. A gigolo has to be faithful and satisfied with his lot. You'd be running after the kitchenmaid too and that would be your mistake. To be a gigolo requires a sense of

discipline, of dedication. All trades have their ethics. A gigolo, Mark, feels no desires other than the desire to rot away in silk pants for the rest of his life. You wouldn't be able to have your cake and eat it.

– You've got something there.
– But be frank. Have you ever done an honest day's work in your life?
– You're under a delusion, mate, Mark said. When I'm work- ing I'm nothing but a slave. A slave. Go on the stage yourself. Get a bucketful. Len's got a hidden hoard. We'll put you on the road.
– No thanks.
– Why not? They'd lap you up.
– I'd die in a week. Quite frankly, when I think of the English dramatic heritage and then look around me at the crowd of poofs and ponces that support it I feel like throwing in the sponge.
– But you're not even in the ring. I'm the one who has to put up with it.
– Yes, I suppose you do.
– You're damn right.

Smoke from the cigarettes mingled above the table, sliding to the windowpane. Mark crossed his legs, the table jolted, the water in the flowerbowl swayed. He blew a path through the smoke.

– A funny thing happened to me last night, Len said.
– What?
– I squashed a tiny insect while I was doing some math- ematics. And I brushed the remains off my finger with my thumb, without thinking about it. Then I realized that the fragments were growing like fluff. As they were falling, they were becoming larger, like fluff. I had put my hand into the body of a dead bird.
– What mathematics were you doing? Mark asked.
– Geometry.
– There's your answer.

– Anyway, Len said, I made a decision on the strength of it. I've decided to go over to Paris next week.

– Paris? Pete said. What for?

– How can I tell you what for?

– Alone? Mark asked.

– No. With a bloke at Euston. An Austrian. He pops backwards and forwards. It's an open invitation. He's got a room there.

– But what do you want to go to Paris for? Pete asked.

– Why shouldn't he? said Virginia.

– You don't understand, Ginny. We've got Len's interests at heart. Haven't we, Len?

– What?

– No, Pete said, you're quite entitled to go to Paris if you want to. It's just that I wouldn't do it myself, that's all. I take it you don't look upon it as a holiday?

– No, I suppose not. On the other hand...

– I thought you were going to get another job here.

– I'll take a return ticket, Len said. I might return within the hour. Who knows?

– Well, drop us a card, Mark said.

Virginia stood up, smoothing her dress.

– I think I'll go for a walk in the garden, she said.

– I admit, of course, that Paris has never meant much to me.

– I know what you mean. But you can never tell.

– I'll come with you, Mark said. Show you the lilac.

Len looked up.

– Come with me?

– Not you.

– It doesn't altogether ring true, Paris, Pete said.

Mark and Virginia walked over the lawn and stood under the arch of the lilactree.

– I like this tree.

– Mind, Mark said, catching her arm. Spider's web.

– I didn't see it.

- That is a beautiful dress.
- Yes.
- A man of many talents.
She plucked a leaf and pressed it to her mouth.
- Yes.
- How's school?
- Fine.
- Do you still like the kids?
- Yes, of course.
- And they like you?
- I think so.
- Your arms are very brown.
- We went into the country the other day. The kids and me.
  We went to Kent.
He leaned against a bough.
- Yes?
- Mmn.
- Well, how's Marie Saxon?
- She said to tell you she's managed to forget you.
- Sweet.
- She said it was a hard job but her heart has healed.
- What a shame.
- Is it?
- I believe in hopeless love.
- You do?
- No, it's not a shame. It's nothing.
She tore the leaf across, along the spine.
- What do you do with yourself? she asked.
- This and that.
- This and what?
- Depends which way the wind's blowing.
- Which way has it been blowing?
- I can't really remember. What about you?
- Me?
- Yes.
- In the pink. Let's go in.

They walked back across the lawn.

- What I mean is, Shakespeare didn't need to go further than his own front door.
- But if someone had given him a ticket, would he have said no?
- No, I suppose not.
- They may drive me out, Len said. They may not even let me in.
- Well, I wouldn't worry, Pete said. You must have a liberal stock of false noses by now.
- What about a stroll? Mark said.
- Yes. Good idea.

They walked out of the house and across the road towards Hackney Downs. Mark bought a paper and turned to the back page.

- See one of these books I've got here? Pete said, pointing to the small pile in the crook of his arm. Very interesting. About surgery in Elizabethan times. Do you know a woman once gave birth to six puppies?
- No! Len said.
- Hutton's made a century against Essex, Mark said.
- He can't do anything right these days, can he? Len said.
- How did she manage it? Mark said.
- Well, the point about these puppies, Pete said, is that she kept them in a pig's bladder under her chastity blanket.

Mark threw the paper over a wall.

- For Jesus Christ's fucking sake! Pete screamed, hurling the books at Virginia's feet, will you stop walking between those fucking paving stones? You're driving me mad!
- Bastard! What do you mean? Bastard!
- I'll kill you, you fucking bitch, if you don't stop it!

Their screams pitched and grated together. Virginia, breathless, stared at his face. A silence hummed. Turning, she walked slowly on. Pete picked up the books and he, Mark and Len continued behind her.

– Well, if I don't see you before you go, Len, Pete said, look after yourself in Paris.

– I'll probably see you before I go.

– Yes.

They reached the beginning of the Downs. Virginia, ahead of them, had stopped under a tree. Pete paused by the railings.

– I'll be seeing you, he said.

– Yes, Mark said.

Len and Mark walked back along the road. In the afternoon quiet they heard Virginia sobbing. Mark looked back and saw her crouched in Pete's arms. He stopped to light a cigarette, drawing carefully. He looked back. They were moving slowly under the avenue of trees, on to the grass. He watched them move across the field, and out of sight.

– Are you coming?

Sixteen

They've gone on a picnic. They've time for picnics. They've left me to sweep the yard, to pacify the rats. No sooner do they leave, these dwarfs, than in come the rats. They've left me to attend to the abode, to make their landscape congenial. I can't do a good job. It's a hopeless task. The longer they stay the greater the mess. Nobody lifts a finger. Nobody gets rid of a damn thing. All their leavings pile up, pile mixing with pile. When they return from their picnics I tell them I've had a clearance, that I've been hard at it since their departure. They nod, they yawn, they gobble, they spew. They don't know the difference. In truth, I sit and stir the stumps, the skins, the gristle. I tell them I've slaved like a martyr, I've skivvied till I was black in the face, what about a tip, what about a promise of a bonus, what about a little something? They yawn, they show the blood stuck between their teeth, they play their scratching game, they tongue their chops, they bring in their nets, their webs, their traps, they make monsters of their innocent catch, they gorge. Countless diversions. What about the job? What about the job in hand? After all my devotion. What about the rats I dealt with? What about the rats I saved for you, that I plucked and hung out to dry, what about the ratsteak I tried all ways to please you? They don't touch it, they don't see it. Where is it, they hidden it, they're hiding it till the time I can no longer stand upright and I fall, they'll bring it out then, grimed then, green, varnished, rigid, and eat it as a victory dish.

Seventeen

Pete walked along the east bank of the river. Under the wood-yard wall he stopped, peering.

Cow's skull. Taken to root. No. A boulder. Dead lump of brass, battered.

Battlements of white wood jawed over the wall, clamped in frames of iron.

Palms of iron, upturned, manacled.

Deathmask of ironwood struck shadowed across the water.

A penny for the old guy.

He winked at the one star.

Only one this shift. Rest given up the ghost.

The jut of wood grunted, crisp, shaved, splintered. His heel grated gravel and dust. On to hard stone, the slope of the bridge. On the bridge's hump he stared the river and wide reach of dark. Collected, rolled, let out. The yolk of gob flattened and sang white to a slap on the surface.

King of the horsefly world. Enemy in the knee.

Ah. Some worm's a traitor in my camp.

Distance it.

His eyes glinted the boulder's head on the bank.

Pawnbroker's ball, carbuncled.

He descended to the bankpath and squatting, scrabbled in the dark under of the stone, wrenched it out of dirt. Beetles capered in the yawn. He swung the boulder. A crash, a swallow of water.

Fined thirty bob.

The river jolted, hollowed, fell from his boot. Through sliteyes he watched the slicing fall of a gull. The bird landed on pebble, padding to probe in the mud. Silently Pete moved along the shore. The gull tugged at the corpse, feet in its mouth. With a snap the cloth of the rat's head tore. The beak dug and pierced.

Dessert. Cheese and biscuits.

His head thumped, he turned and crossed the bridge. The fields spread out of sight and dark.

Dead as a squashed bug.

His eardrum pricked the muffle of sound, the beat.

Hold hard.

A long boat lunged a brisk pulse, along his course, past him, on the water; sucked under the bridge, stroked swift upstream. The wash stirred back, squabbling on pebble.

Athletes. Hold on. Animal in my gut. Knee argument.

Quick. Get on.

Dust in the fairground crackled and swam. The stalls ticked in the dark, shuttered.

Sweat still running. Arena sweat. Is this it?

Keep a straight line.

In the sweat of night a shunting engine cranked, stopped short. Heat of the merrygoround needled to his throat.

Knock at this gypsy door. Ask for remission.

Ask for the other exit.

A glut of bile creased into his mouth.

This is it.

Heavylegged walking he reached the lock. The river became canal.

Knee won't make. Labour of birth. Gaswork now. Settle it. Steady. Hold. Would you I am?

His hand pounded staccato on the iron rail. A stab shook sauntering through his joints. Knees bent, he clutched, crouched, struck icy in the eyes.

Wash black wash black.

He summoned a grip.

Knuckle.

A clout slapped his nape, scrawled a blot of cold over his skull.

Now.

His eyelid snapped a stone down.

Father.

Yes now you're the one dear only son only the open blood canal the only night and the one taped to be taped. What choking spit and the ornaments the makeshift grass the splintered grass. A riderless horse canal turn blowing. Blowing bubbles I am the only so the only son. Belay there to stern. Rind no yes ammonia. My throat his only rubbished son. Black all to iron. So this rust. Rust and one. Yes now you're done and made the one dear one. Split knifestalks yellow under green the nightblades crust and silk. At the canal turn. Bitch gone black. Steel and bland. Forge I hammer I blood to forge that ice.

No hand. Gaswork top and flat. Steel dish for such my only loss. Glass how can you to the grit? Eyeball sum up in wax. To say so. To say no. To pull and parley I chat I am swabbed to now. God and his leak. Cocaine Christ. Now. Bolt. Which now lock? Mains check check mains a blowout call them in call them check no bolt. Blowlamp now. Put so put on list. Steel of steel sweat current a current to yes to again. Concrete grass shoots grey no. No price no bid. No bid no board no chalk no sale no room no place no sign no tack cold cage carbolic summer.

Alone to be alone. Shiver me out. Douse down seeing. Taped to be so. Good and all. Time about. Barge. Old sows. Water in heat. Blindabout only existing son. No barter. Closed shop at the metal crack. Yes and I know it to that. That's all. Am I your nighwatchman? All aboard. So to see. A breather. Screw this hinge. That's it. Cobblers on. Air so. Keep the change. Compliments of. Air now. Now tread now back. Can move. Shall move.

Eighteen

Len climbed the stone stairs, in the echo of his steps. He walked along the balcony and stopped at the door. It was ajar. He went in. There was no sound in the flat. The hallway was dark. A crack of light shone from the kitchen.

– Pete?

There was no reply. Len walked to the kitchen door and looked in. Pete was sitting upright in an armchair by the window, facing him, in his shirtsleeves. Len stepped into the room. He rested his hand upon the dresser and thumbed the edge.

– The emissary, Pete said, smiling.

– What do you mean?

– That's another question, Pete said. I'm talking about yachts. He moved his arms slowly to the arms of the chair.

– They're as clean as a whistle. They have balance and proportion. They're a logical unit. That's the only thing to look for in this world. Logic. Logic in a drainpipe. Logic in a leaf.

His frame shivered. He gripped the chairarms.

– Virginia has put on lipstick and gone out with a girlfriend. A day off. I'm glad. She's easily frightened. So you're here? You've stepped over the mat, into this room. I can't quibble now. I suspend belief. Cockeyed. I'll take it that you're here. I won't abolish you. I know who you're not, anyway. That is something decisive. No. To say I have a screw loose would not be accurate. On the contrary, my screws are so tight they grind against each other from each side of my cranium. It's a music I respect. Certainly. You could say that if you smell impending lunacy you're bound to recruit enough moral force to combat such a disaster. You would be right. But tonight not. I have made my way home from the canal. The mind has slipped its leash. Without my

110

warrant. Acting on its own volition. I am no longer in charge. Or to what extent? There is no obsession here, only bereavement. I resent that. There is no need for you to pray yet. If you slip on to your knees and pray I shall be mortally insulted. It would be a prayer for the dead. That surprises you. How could you see me as a corpse? Quite right. I am a living man of extreme potential. A force to be reckoned with. A force who can reckon with forces, who reckoned with the devil and therefore created him. How are your negotiations? Where are you? My trouble is, I'm valid. That's not your concern.

Pete winked his right eye.

– I'm nattering like a clubman. To the white meat. I can't see you. You're insubstantial to the point of chaos. Order in all things. I'm the only logical unit you know. The one you'd do better not to know. But of course I can keep distance. Distance is child's play. Perhaps it is kept for me. Where does distance end? I can't sidestep the facts, though I admit to alter the fact of distance might be desirable. Love is easy in the nursery. And life can only be kept with a tape-measure. If so, so what? The world sucks on these irrelevances. That measure may be a slug is irrelevant. And pride is a grotesque irrelevance. To do homage to it is suicide. Did you know that? By bits. First, you slit your eyelids. With a pincer you pluck your toenails. The rest follows. Such a course of events ceases to be eventful, it becomes method, simple procedure. Procedure is simple when suicide has set in. Are you still here? Because suicide itself is irrelevant. It is as constructive to upset the chamber-pot. I do not participate and never will. Neither in their chamberpots nor in their procedure. I wrote their scriptures. I trod their scriptures before them. I am of a mind to abdicate. When my sense of distance has been proved wrong. And no one but me can eliminate it. When I have proved distance malleable I shall lay down this sword. Got to prove they exist, then lay down the sword. Because I am the axiom I will

111

not escape. In the act of proof, after all, is the proof. The gaschamber, I won't deny it, is a ripe and purposive unit. I look into my garden and see walking blasphemies. A blasphemy is a terrible thing. They cut the throat of a child over the body of a naked woman. The blood runs down her back, the blood runs between the cheeks of her arse. In my sight the world commits sacrilege. I shall walk to my own coffin, when I have chosen to make time. Soon I shall place a tombstone upon that world. The odour adds too much of disease to my own disease at present. The whole matter must be turned over to God and he can carry the can back. In time. In his own time. But I shall of course put the matter to him. Let it never be said God is unreasonable. I see you as clearly as a cheesecake. The world is vanity. The world is impertinent. I must cease to belong. My own bile is my own bile that has been placed in my mouth. And I give warrant to the worm. It has been necessary. My soul is old, I am the beginner in this world. My virtue is in the appraisal of my worms. I have forced them into the no-man's-land of my own dictate. I have located their nest and acted accordingly. They are my dependants. They exist only by virtue of me. When I die, they are dead. But since I have located the place I can act from faith. I can afford to be flexible. I can move on many fronts. And I am a mainroad man, there's no point in doubting it. I must keep to that course, however much pus congeals. Amen to all the good souls. I cannot deviate. My immediate and upper authority would frown. There's the point. Such action would prove incongruous with my birthright. I would not be what I am. I see you now but can you see my existing head? That visage has blessed many innocents, nodding. But though I can feel it, now, on my neck, I do not believe you can see it. For I tear a hole in my skull with every word I speak. Each syllable suffocates a gut. Standing in one room I touch the framework of a larger. What is ludicrous is that I am too big for my ideas. But that's all in the frame and I despise it and it shall be

done until the balance is achieved and then I shall present
my terms and my own scales shall weigh them. I am my
own saviour. All the world knows that. Now what is it? It's
quite all right. Quite all right. I'm as gentle as a lamb. And
you look as though you'd seen a ghost.

Len stepped away from the dresser and sat down at the table.

– What do you want? Pete said.

– Nothing.

Pete sat forward and began to raise himself from the chair.

– What do you want? Len said, starting up.

– I want a glass of water.

– I'll get it, Len said, going to the sink.

– Thanks, Pete said.

He watched Len turn the tap, took the glass and drank.

– Thanks.

Len placed the glass on the drainingboard and sat down. Pete
licked his lips.

– What was your idea, he asked, in coming here?

– I thought I'd pop in.

Pete closed his eyes.

– What time is it?

– Threeish.

– In my jacket there, Pete said, you'll find a cigarette. Throw
   it over, will you?

Len felt in a pocket, brought out a cigarette, and passed it.

– Here's some matches, he muttered, taking a box from his
   pocket.

– I didn't know you smoked.

– I don't.

– I don't think I have any more.

Pete lit the cigarette and let the match burn in the ashtray.

– I am ill, he said.

– Yes.

Len pocketed his matches.

– I wonder if you know what I lack?

– What?

– What would you say?

Len frowned and bent his head.

– I don't know.

– I lack guts, Pete said.

– I wouldn't say that.

– Yes. I lack guts.

– Do you?

– You mustn't think, Pete said, that I don't know what you and Mark are. I do. I recognize you both.

– Me? Mark? What do you mean? What are we?

– I take it you are my friends.

Len grimaced and clipped his palm under his jaw.

– Yes.

– Why don't you ask me, Pete said, if I recognize Virginia?

– Why should I ask you that?

– If you want to know another thing, I'll tell you. Because I lack guts, I commit spite. I suffer under that bondage. I commit spite at all corners, and in the face of the image.

He drew on his cigarette.

– Do you know what that makes me?

– It makes you Shammes to the Pope of China, Len said.

– Very true.

– What else?

– That could be it, I admit.

Len took off his glasses and examined them.

– What's it like out now? Pete asked.

– It's dark now.

– Have you ever met the Pope of China?

– Yes.

– What's he like?

– He's like you.

– No, I'm his Shammes.

– You're also the Pope of China.

– No. That's where you're wrong, Pete said. I'm not. If I may say so, that is a gross error on your part.

– Yes, I see that.

114

- And has also been on my part.
He stood up.
- Air.
- Where are you going? Len asked.
- Outside.
They walked out to the balcony and leaned over it. Len put his glasses into his pocket and rubbed his eyes.
- My eyes are very bad, he said. Now I've taken off my glasses, I can see.
- That's reasonable.
- Isn't that the moon up there? It must be late, Len said. Can you see the lights there, on the roads? All that. They're bells. They have that sound. I can see the moon where I stand. It's all right. The globe's turning. This is not night. This isn't night. It's the globe turning. Can you hear the moon? Eh? And these lights? There's a bell here. We're making this bell. We're making the light. Can you hear the moon, through the sound? It is in us.

Nineteen

- The world's got nothing on me, Mark said. Where's the bother?
- You're a marked man, said Len.
- Possibly. Marked but indifferent.
- Would you be indifferent to the torturing wheel? Pete asked.
- Oh no.
- So you're not indifferent to everything? asked Virginia.
- All I'm trying to say is that everything's a calamity, Mark said. There are items within the fact of that fact that I am unable to accept. But I accept that I can't accept them. I accept that which I can't accept. I accept the fact within which I act. In other words I carry on merrily.
- It does me good to hear it, Pete said. But, on the other hand, everything's not a calamity. There are certain kinds of achievement, which are, to say the least of it, worthwhile.
- Are there?
- Your uncle must have been Chief Rabbi, Len said.
- Why?
- Why? You're steeped in Talmudic evasion!
- What did the Talmud ever evade?
- How do I know? I've never read it, as such.
- As such, Pete said, yes.
- In that case, you're entitled to make that statement, Mark said. You're not prejudiced. I haven't read it either. We can both afford to be objective.
- I mean, from some points of view you could even be called an achievement yourself, Pete said.
- I can't deny it. But I'm only an achievement within the larger calamity, I keep telling you.
- You're very chirpy tonight, Len said.

– Do you enjoy life? said Virginia.

– Up to the neck, Mark said. But I don't ask questions.

– It's a funny old world we live in, Pete said.

They sat.

– You're looking very well today, Ginny, said Len.

– I'm feeling it.

– Every time, said Mark.

– Make me a willow whatsaname at your gate, Pete said.

– And call upon my howdoyoudo within the house, said Mark.

– That's it.

– What does she say to that? Mark asked.

– Olivia?

– Yes.

– You might do much, Virginia said.

It was growing darker. She collected the cups and took them into the kitchen.

– I'll wipe them up, Mark said, following her.

– When are you off, Len? Pete said.

– Tomorrow.

– Look. Here's a couple of quid. Might come in handy.

– No, that's all right.

– Take it.

– All right. Thanks.

– I wouldn't mind making a trip myself, Pete said.

– Why don't you?

– I will one day. But it'll be farther off.

Mark opened the backdoor and chased a cat through the fence. He threw a stone through the lilacarch. She watched him. Before her, through the broad windows, summer leaned into the room with the last lights of day. The setting sun muzzed along the lilacblossom.

– Lovely evening, he said.

– It is.

– Where's the wiper?

– Let me do it. You go back.

– Sure?

– Yes.

She rinsed the crockery and placed it on the drainingboard. She then walked out into the garden. Under the boughs of the tree she looked up. Through the array of darkgreen the sky chinked, a needle of light before the dusk. She moved through a tangle of weed to the wall, webbed and tightleafed. The sky planed down along the houses. In a stepping silence the dusk converged about her. Her footfall disturbed the brush. A grip of red flaked the skyrim. This then was the world altering. Lightly she touched the treestalks and shivering, clasped her arms, the red fading, and the light. Shades ducked by the upper fence. She moved to where they hunched, below the black tree, closed with them and stood still. She propped her arms upon the fence, the wood grating her elbows. She covered her face.

– Virginia.

Pete walked over the grass and through the lilacarch.

– What are you doing?

– Watching it get dark.

He drew her back to him and pressed her breasts.

– Ginny –

– It's cold.

He turned her to him and looked at her.

– Is it?

Virginia looked into his eyes.

– Yes.

– What are they up to out there? Mark asked. Should I tell them I possess the best bed in Hackney?

Len did not answer.

– The world's full of surprises, Mark said.

He walked to the bookshelf and banged two books back into place.

– Well, he said, it's all in the way you tie your tie. Here's a book. Thomas Aquinas. Never read a word of it. Am I better off or worse off?

118

– Worse.

Mark sat down.

– I dropped a beggar a bob the other day.

– What does that mean?

– Means what it is.

– What is it?

– A bobsworth, Mark said.

– You're straining at the leash, Len said.

– Straining at the leash?

– That's what it looks like.

– What leash?

– I only know you're straining.

– You're off the mark.

Virginia and Pete came into the room.

– We're off, he said.

– Uh-huh.

– I watched the night arrive, she said.

– Very nice too, said Mark.

– I can't do that, Len said.

– Why not? she asked.

– No. Impossible. I can't look at the sky.

– Works wonders sometimes, Pete said.

– What's there to it? Mark said. First it's day, then it's night.
Granted.

– Mother nature? Pete said. I thought you were partial. Well,
watch yourself in Paris, Len.

– I will.

– Have a good time, said Virginia.

– Thanks.

– Keep in touch, said Pete.

– I will.

– Be seeing you Pete, said Mark.

– Yes. Cheerio.

– Cheerio, said Virginia.

– Cheerio, said Mark.

– Cheerio, said Len.

Twenty

Easy come easy go. They are not bothered, these dwarfs. As it should be. They are never at a loss, never at a loose end. The tiniest substances, the prettiest trifles, nourish and sustain them. Now there is a new game, to do with beetles and twigs. There is a rockery of redhot cinder. The hairs are curly and oiled on their necks. Always squatting and bending, dipping their wicks in the custard. Home methods are the best.

I stand wafted by odours, in the shadows. From time to time a lick of flame screws up their nostrils. They yowl, they scutter to the sandpit, pinch, dribble, chew, whimper, gouge, then soothe each other's orifices with a local ointment, and then, all gone, all forgotten, they lark about, each with his buddy, get out the nose spray, the scented syringe, settle down for the night with ginger beer and a doughnut.

Twenty-one

- You're a strange boy, said Sonia.
- Am I really?
- Yes.
- Give me your glass.

They edged through the crowd to the table.

- How am I strange? said Mark. Go on. Tell me.

Now I combed her hair, even manicured her fingernails.

- Don't you know him? Pete said. Big dark bloke, over by the bar.
- No, I don't, said Brenda.
- Oh yes, said Pete, he's a very old pal of mine.
- Really?
- Yes. Met him in a Turkish bath. Never looked back since. Drink up and we'll dance.

- All right, said Mark, I admit it. I'm very strange.

I heard something moaning in my corner, I tried my best to see.

- I am, there's no getting away from it, exceedingly strange.

It was the mother bedbug, coming for to eat me.

The couples crawled and slid to the beat in the crossed lights of the wall lamps.

- Well, said Pete, this is luxury pure and simple. Oops. This Elaine has plenty of money, eh?
- It's Baxter, said Brenda. It's his flat.

- Oh yes, I forgot. This is a concubinary.
- A what?
- A state of affairs, said Pete. A particular set of circum-
  stances obtaining in a particular place at a particular time.
  The only moral in that is that you can't be too particular.
- What do you do, anyway, if you're not an actor?
- If you really want to know, let's sit down a minute.
- I like the way you dance.
- You know what this is? he said, leading her to the window.
  It's a caper. Not only that. I've never smelt so many odours
  in my life. Perfume at war. The suppliance of a minute and
  so on. Hold here and I'll get a drink.

- Oh don't think you can pull that old one on me.
- What old one?
- Looking at my mouth like that, said Sonia. Don't be so
  bloody studied.
- Me!
- Don't shout.
- Me studied! Mark said.
- Now you're angry.
- Why shouldn't I be angry?
- You think I'm repulsing you.
- Think! Think! scowled Mark. I think. You think. He thinks.
- I don't know, Pete said, pouring a drink, thinking got me
  into this.
- And thinking's got to get you out.
- I doubt it.
- Sonia, Pete, said Mark.
- Got you into what? said Sonia.
- Bad habits, said Pete.
- Now is grown the very habit of my soul, said Mark.

I can get any woman's man in town, I can stand him up or lay
him down.

- Mark's making the most of it.
- So are you, said Brenda.
- Christmas comes but once a year.

- Who is Pete?
- Apalomine.
- A member of your clan?
- A member? He's the witchdoctor.
- What are you?
- The hangman. But there'll be a new election in the autumn.
- Really?
- And then, Mark said, who can tell? We might all be looking for new jobs.
- Look, said Sonia, are you going to dance? Or I'll get some-one who will.

I know that you know that you know that I know.

- All right, if you want the truth, I'm doing literary research at Cambridge University for students.
- How fascinating, said Brenda. Literary research? But what do you do?
- Do? Pete said. I dig up old manuscripts and give my honest and respected opinion.
- No?
- Yes. Dig, dig. Between you and me – and this is really top secret – you won't let it out?
- No, really. What?
- We've got a special permit to open graves.
- Graves?
- Coffins, Pete said. Tombs. You never know what they've taken down with them, these people.
- Like Egyptian mummies.
- That's right, Pete said. Ever seen a corpse?

- Mark! called Elaine.

– What?

He turned sharply and fell over. The dancers scattered. Sonia, two men and Elaine helped him to his feet.

– All right, all right.

– You looked ten! Elaine said. Didn't he, darling?

– Did you call my name? Mark said.

– Yes. What's the Greek god's name? I've forgotten.

– His name is Pete.

– He's a witchdoctor, said Sonia.

– Will he treat me?

– No, Pete said, mostly they sat on 'em. You've got to lift up the pelvisbone with a pair of tweezers. Big tweezers. Can't leave fingermarks, you see. Canon law. Well, under the arse it's even money you'll find a priceless manuscript. Sometimes, on the other hand, they've tied them round the man's limbs, but the flesh takes no time to rot, so it isn't much trouble to get them off. One job we did, the manuscripts were fixed by a chain to the bloke's ankle. We had to send home for a screwdriver to unbolt the nuts. Drink up. The biggest shock I ever had was when a skeleton collapsed on top of me and nearly bit my ear off. I had a curious sensation at that moment. I thought I was the skeleton and he was my longlost uncle come to kiss me goodnight. When my mate hauled me out I felt like Lazarus raised from the dead. Ever felt that? No, well of course you've never been inside a grave. You should try it. I recommend it, honest, I mean if you want to taste everything life has to offer. Oh well, you'll be inside one one day, won't you? Unless you're going to be cremated. Or drowned at sea. I'll tell you what, if you fancy it, I'll work a fiddle and take you along to my next cemetery job. It'll be worth your while. You look like a ghost, as it is. That's your attraction. Death is a crafty customer. But not entirely without virtues, when you come down to it. Yes, my job, taking it all in all, is not uninteresting. What do you think?

Oh now I'm discontented, now I'm discontented here.

- Oh balls, said Elaine, of course it's a lovely party. What's to stop it? Baxter's loaded. But I'm thinking of going into the Park, on the game. I really am.
- You'll do all right, Mark said.

She paused by a seated man.

- How are you, Don?

He stood and rested against them.

- How many times have you been shagged in the last week? he asked.
- You must never, Elaine husked, closing her eyes and swaying against them both, never, use that word. You must say fucked. It is the only word that becomes a lady.
- I don't care what I say, said Don. When's my turn?
- It will come, said Elaine, through sliteyes. Your turn will come. Patience. I had two doctors the other night. In one bed.
- You bitch, said Don.
- General practitioners? Mark asked.

- Well, Pete said, there are occupations and occupations. What's your occupation?
- You know, said Brenda, stroking his hair.
- You enact. Ever played Mistress Overdone?
- Who?
- Had nine husbands. All done in plastic. Trick lighting. It's all a matter of the old optique. Either you've got it or you haven't got it. Philosophy doesn't come into it. Leave that to the wet weather.

Put me in your big brass bed and roll me till I'm cherry red.

- I am an actor, Mark said, only nor-nor-west. When the wind is southerly –
- Well? said Sonia.

125

– I know a whore from a giblet.

You go to my head, like a bubble in a glass of champagne.

– I'm going blind, Mark said. Can't you open a window?
– Are you rooted to this spot? Pete said, pouring drinks.
– Where there's a bar there's a way.
– Hello, smiled Elaine. I'm your hostess.
– This is a good party.
– Where did you get such curly hair?
– Work of God.
– This man has the most extraordinary occupation, said Brenda, sipping.
– He gropes for trout in a peculiar river, said Mark, collapsing into a chair.
– Can I have a lock of your hair? asked Elaine.
– All rights reserved, Pete said. Sorry.

I went down to St James Infirmary, saw my baby there.

– You weren't going to tell her what I did, were you?
– Why?
– I told you. It's top secret. Over to the window. Excuse us.
They sat down.
– Look, Pete said. They're in a mist. Hell's third circle. Do you like this life?
– I like you, she whispered, kissing him.
– Mind yourself. Look out of this window. London's flat out on her back. It's a laughing matter. What time is it?
– Kiss me. Now.

– Upstairs, Mark muttered. Downstairs. Upstairs. In my lady's chamber. Where are my switzers!
– Shut up!
– Who said that?
– Shut up, said Elaine, on Don's arm. You're drunk and dreary.

126

– Thank you.

Mean to me, how can you be so mean to me?

- The point is, Pete said, women are women. It doesn't do to forget it.
- No, it doesn't.
- Errors, errors. Nonrecognition. It's a capital offence. They've left me to prosecute myself. And I'll tell you what. I haven't got a leg to stand on.
- I'm a woman, said Brenda.
- You? What makes you say that?
- You don't think I'm a virgin?
- Mind how you go, Pete said. If I fall, we all fall.
- Don't drink so much.
- Dignity! Dignity! said Mark, looming.
- Sit down or stand up.
- You can't have too much of it, said Mark, veering away.

Baby, baby, take your big fat legs off me. It may be sending you honey, but it's beating hell out of me.

- Come in here, said Sonia.
- What?
- In here.
- Here?
- Here's some coffee.
- This is a kitchen, Mark said.
- Drink it.
- Too bright. Who made it?
- Take a sip.
The door opened and a man and a girl rushed in.
- Where's the bin?
They seized the rubbishbin and emptied its contents on to the floor. The man then gripped the bin upside down between his thighs and, waddling to the door, the girl goosing him,

tomtomed across the hall into the gameroom. The door swung shut. Mark skated through eggshells, potatopeel and baconrind to Sonia and kissed her.

– Before you love me, he said, you must learn to run through snow, leaving no footprint.
– Drink it.
– It's a Turkish proverb.

– Gather round, boys!
Elaine jumped on a chair, skirt at her waist.
– I promised!
She moaned and wriggled to the music, suspenders tight. The crowd humped together, squealing, around her, to the floor; the room plapped into halflight, low from two wall lamps, glowing on her legs, over the ducking heads.
– A ballet for you, she grated.
– Do you like her from this angle?
– Come outside, Pete said.
– Now!
The skirt swung and floated.
– Aaaaaaaaah!
Mark gaped the crisp and shutter of light under his eyelid. Elaine stepped down. By a wall lamp she swayed, slipping off her blouse.
– This is my party.
– Do you like her? Would you like her? asked Sonia.
– Catch it!
Her brassière flipped into the dark.

– Put me, baby, put me in your big brass bed.

She danced alone from shade to light by the wall. Cackles broke, snuffed. The floor beat time. She caressed her breasts. She slid her hands down her briefs to her buttocks, turning. A figure through the shadows pulled her to him. They fell. Mark trod on a glass, staggered by the bar. He clutched to Sonia. They sat. The sofa sonked.

Give me a pigfoot and a bottle of gin, slay me cause I'm in my sin. Slay me cause I'm full of gin.

The room grunted, slapped. Light whimpered across the bodies. Aayi! cried Elaine, I'm dying. Aaaah, said Mark, God knows. Baxter beat on the wall. Slay me slay me slay slay moaning in my corner you go to my head beating hell out of me I know that you know that any woman's man mean to me why are you so legs off me I'm full of there saw my baby roll me cherry pigfoot roll me red.

– Outside.

Mark jolted the room from the rolling shapes, he and Sonia stumbled into the red hall.

– Here.

He pushed at a door, they closed inside.

– Here.

The bed slumped. He pulled.

– Hey? Blimey.

Pete and Mark sat up, cocked heads, regarded.

– Well, Mark said.

– Well.

– How's business?

– Mustn't grumble.

– Bit cramped in this gaff.

– Too true.

– Not a very efficient idea, this.

Sonia pulled away and walked to the door.

– Wait for me, said Brenda.

The door cracked, pale heads whispered through dark, the red light damaged the black, shut.

– You been doing your bit for democracy?

– My flag's at halfmast, Pete said. What about you?

– I'm past it.

– Well, what about getting out of here?

– Yes, let's get out of here.

Twenty-two

Look. The moon and the black leaves. I am smelling it out. The bright day is done. My slow dying dead, my dead dying slow, so long in its tooth. That's the character of it, gentlemen. I am in a nunnery. He has managed to banish me. What he hoped and what he feared. Oh very near the mark. The who? That's beside the point. Which is quite another thing, distinct, shall I say, from the main issue, from the one pressing and deplorable conundrum. A country train will take you there. I have taken the hint. Shame on all things. I am a bat. He wasn't free with his booze. That did it. I shall throw my hand in. Chuck it all in. Scrub round it. Under stealth I lived, under stealth I'll leave. A new order. The fires. The land is black. There's a blackness on my lids. I am blind.

And now you have come, now at this time have found it is time, it is no longer so. I am cold with the years of you. You came to me in that garden. I told you I was cold. You knew what I said. I am a bat. I must not be a bat. I shall leave you.

Twenty-three

– Shakespeare! Pete exclaimed, placing his mug with a thump
on the table, what was Shakespeare? Only a jobbing play-
wright. A butcher's boy with a randy eye. And yet he made
his point. You know what you look like when you drink
that beer? A porpoise with all its suckers working.
– That's it, Mark said. Where these people go wrong is in
trying to give him a name and number. Every so often
someone decides he needs a change of underwear. What
they don't realize is that he's dressed for all weathers and
he can smell them a mile off. They think he can swing their
case if they offer him a percentage of the profits. They hope
he'll turn King's evidence in their favour. It's all a lot of
onion. He's never attempted to cut anyone's losses, least of
all his own.
– Very true.
– He doesn't go round with a needle and thread, Mark said,
or a tenday cure. When does he attempt to sew up the
wound, or reshape it?
– What you're saying is that he's not a moral poet.
– A moral poet? If you mean by that that he doesn't canvass
for one kind of plug as opposed to another, then I'm bloody
sure he isn't. If I said that then that's what I'm saying.
Drink up and we'll have another one on moral plugs that
bottle up the sink. What do you mean by morality?
– I'll tell you, Pete said. I've been doing quite a bit of thinking
myself about this business. The way I look at it is this. Isn't
morality as we use the term the practice of good towards
your fellows? A responsibility we have to assume where we
are simply social creatures. But it's only a convenience
suited to the needs of a given situation, at a given time, in a

given place. It goes no way towards solving, do you know what I mean, the problem of good and evil, which is adjacent to any intelligent morality.

– What do you mean?

– Well, I don't see how good and evil can be defined by contemplation of the results of particular actions. Good is a productive state of mind, if you like, as well as a social virtue. But a productive state of mind in some circumstances may become a sterile one in others. Good and evil, they're both qualified by circumstances. As chemicals, they're neither arbitrary nor static.

– Give me your can, Mark said.

He walked to the bar and returned with two best bitters.

– Cheers.

– Leave Hamlet out of it. He's another story. But the others, Othello, Macbeth and Lear, are men whose great virtues are converted by their very superfluity into faults. Do you see what I mean? Othello is jealous because of an excess of love. But look at it. He was in love only so long as his affections were unhampered by the necessity to explain them. Lear's extreme of magnanimity starts the landslide. Macbeth's real trouble was that he thought too much of his wife. The trouble with these people is that they refuse to recognize their own territorial limitations. Their feelings are in excess of the facts. All they're doing is living beyond their means. And when they have to act, not upon their notions but upon their beliefs, they're found to be lacking. When they're called to account by common justice they're wrong. At the same time, of course, they're right. They're right according to our admiration and sympathy. But that's to look at them in no way morally.

– What are we sympathizing with?

– We're sympathizing with what they are when unhampered by the responsibility of action. The necessity of action smothers their virtue. They cease to be morally thinking creatures. Lear, Macbeth and Othello are all forced, in one way or another, to account for what they do and they all fail to do it. Lear and Macbeth don't even attempt to.

The till snapped down and rang through the smoke.

– All they can see is the natural process of cause and effect working in a system of which they have ceased to be a part. They fall away from this system by lack of a social virtue. By not thinking for others. In each case, the initial thinking for others was superficial and unrealized, delusive. Their unique qualities gave them, if you like, the power of dispensation over others. So they thought. Wait a minute. The point, you see, the point is, that as all things are qualified by relevant circumstances, so they considered they were not responsible to a code of morality which did not take them into account. Where these geezers slip up is that they try to overcome a machine of which they remain, whether they like it or not, a part. The machine, if you like, is morality, the standards of the majority. It seems to me that Shakespeare justifies both the man and the machine.

– If he does, how can it be said that he's a moral poet? Mark said, I mean, look what he does. Look at the way he behaves. He never uses a communication cord or a lifebelt, and what's more, he never suggests he's got one handy for your use or his.

– No.

– How can moral judgements be applied when you consider how many directions he travels at once? Hasn't he got enough troubles? Look at what he gets up to. He meets himself coming back, he sinks in at the knees, he forgets the drift, he runs away with himself, he falls back on geometry, he turns down blind alleys, he stews in his own juice, and he nearly always ends up by losing all hands. But the fabric, mate, never breaks. The tightrope is never at less than an even stretch. He keeps in business, that's what, and if he started making moral judgements he'd go bankrupt like the others.

– The point about Shakespeare, Pete said, thumping the

133

table, is that he didn't measure the man up against the idea and give you hot tips on the outcome.

- He wasn't a betting man.
- He laid bare, that's all. I'd defy any man who said he saw good and evil as abstractions. He didn't. Admitted, our own moral sense, such as it is, is likely to be obliterated during these doings. And if you take that obliteration as bad, you can call Shakespeare an immoral poet. But on the other hand, while the experience neutralizes our own morality we must retain some standards by which to measure the whole business. If we had no terms of reference, the experience would be lost.
- Well?
- What takes place is a substitution. We have, instead of common or garden morality – a socio-religious convention depending upon the consent of men to live with each other – we have instead of that the simple fact of man as his own involuntary judge, because as a man of choice he's finally obliged to accept responsibility for his actions. You could say then, that in so far as he points that out, he is a moral poet.
- Ah. So where are we now?
- Back where we started.
- Where's that?
- Back in the booze, Pete said. Come to me when I'm sober. The whole matter's so full of loose ends it gives me heartburn.
- What'll you have?
- Same again.

Pete surveyed the crowded pub, blackgrained and mirrored. Over the head of a redscarfed girl he glimpsed his face in the glass, now blotted out by shifting figures, grazed by smoke, now arrested. Levelly regarding himself, he felt for matches and packet, and lit a cigarette.

- Well, Mark said, placing the mugs on the table, this pub is aware of a visitation tonight.

– Yes, Pete said, the Angel of Death has passed over.

– Did he have one on the house? Cheers.

– You know what, Mark? Good health. You know what your trouble is?

– What's that?

– You want to become a myth.

– A myth is what you make it.

– Shall I tell you the right way to go about it?

– A hot tip, eh?

– Follow me. I am the way and the truth. I am the resurrection and the life.

– I believe you.

– It's gospel, Pete said. When I was born they were waiting on the doorstep with a form for me to fill up. I said I'd accept the job on two conditions.

– What were they?

– First, that I was to have a free hand. I'd send in my reports in my own time.

– What did they say to that?

– Wouldn't give me a straight answer. And they've been queering my pitch ever since.

– It's a carve-up, Mark said. What was the second condition?

– I wanted a worthwhile Judas.

– Well?

– Eh? I haven't met anyone who was quite up to the mark, when all's said and done.

– When is all said and done?

– God has the last word.

– What, with you? I don't believe it.

– God! Pete said. Listen! His stupidity is his own misfortune. If he can't see that I'm the only hope he's got to get him out of the hole he's in, then he deserves nothing else but my contempt. Give me your glass.

He walked to the bar. Mark glimpsed, between faces and shoulders, his own face in the mirror. He concentrated to erase his frown and watched his forehead jolt down, smooth.

- Mind your elbow.
- Did they shower you with dignities, as befits your position? Mark asked.
- Position?
- Aide-de-camp to the Lord. Eh, wait a minute, you must be the Holy Ghost.
- Up your Holy Ghost, Pete said, sitting down. No, the fact of the matter, if you really want to know, is that I'm finished with all that. It was a lark. Look here. I once thought I was a genius. I'm not. I'm a specimen. That's the secret. But I'm prepared, mate, to take myself off the top shelf. I can't see myself for dust. My marketprice is going down. But I'm prepared to recant like a human. The point is, I want living to uphold me. Yes. And another thing, while we're at it. I've said a few rude things about you in the past. And I don't take them back. But the truth's all things. Your faults don't make your virtues any less true.
- I haven't got any faults, Mark said. I am composed of properties and characteristics. No moral blame attached. I have no faults.
- Now now. You can't wash all the blackheads off your face with a statement like that. You might wash your face away. And what would a geezer like you do without a face?
- No bones broken, Mark said.

He lurched to the bar and came back with two double whiskies.
- Hallo, hallo.
- No holds barred, said Mark.
- Well, who shall we toast?
- Let's toast Virginia.
- Right.
- In what fashion?
- Austerely, Pete said. In high simplicity.
- How? What's the order of the sentence?
- To Virginia.
- A textbook toast.

- Why, what do you think?
- Think?
- Any modifications?
- No, I like it.
- All right.
They lifted glasses.
- I think that's a fair toast, don't you?
- It's a textbook toast, Mark said.
- You're right.
- We must drink to Len sometime too.
- We can do that with the beer, Pete said.
- Of course.
- We'll do this one first.
- Right.
- OK.
- Wait a minute, Mark said. We don't touch glasses?
- No. That's elaboration.
- That's true.
- Ready?
- Yes.
They lifted glasses.
- To Virginia.
- To Virginia.
- Good whisky, Pete said.
- Now for Len.
- Yes.
- We can't just say – To Len.
- No, you've got something there.
- That's no good.
- I know, Pete said.
- What?
- To Weinblatt.
- Good enough.
They lifted mugs.
- To Weinblatt.
- To Weinblatt.

137

- I wonder what he's up to now, Mark said.
- Probably sitting on top of the Arc de Triomphe, playing his recorder.
- Do you know where you are at the moment?
- Where?
- In the centre of literary London. The bud of culture.
- All passion spent. It's all a big assumption.
- I'm made of beer.
- And I'll tell you something, Pete said. Space is pure perception. And time is nothing but a formal condition.
- Pete, said Mark, all sorts of things stare me in the face when I wake up in the morning. I can tell you that.
- That's why you can't take no for an answer.
- No is no answer because it's always yes. There's no no. No is nothing and when you're nothing there's no question. No qua no is no and that's that. Otherwise they needn't come and no their noes.
- I'm not going to bid the thunderbearer shoot, Pete said. That was his error.
- He was dropping a clangor which must be dropped.
- It must be dropped, Pete said.

He reached for the mugs and stood up, returning from the bar with two pints.

- You're quite right there, Mark. It must be dropped.
- Have we reached the eighteenth hole yet?
- You're near the waterjump.
- Listen, said Mark, cancel my subscription for next year, will you? I'm resigning.
- There was a poet at the bar, Pete said.
- What did he say to me about you?
- He asked me if I knew who he was.
- Yes?
- I told him he didn't look it.
- Quite right.
- The Rabbi was in bed with his mistress, Pete said, when his landlady knocked on the door. He jumped under the bed,

leaving his bowler hat between the woman's legs. In comes
the landlady. Oy gevalt, she says. The Rabba est aran-
gafelen!

They collapsed at the table.

– Why can you speak Yiddish? Mark asked. Who's the Jew
here, me or you?

– It's the system, Pete said. Do you know there are beautiful
women in this pub?

– Every time. Where's Virginia?

– She's at home.

– At home?

– At her home.

– That's a point.

– Yes, that's the way. I'm beginning to see things.

– See things? That's more than I am.

– I'm breaking through a question, through a false, mate,
hypothesis.

– Don't ask me, Mark said, about the whole business. What
nobody understands is –

– That's all right.

– No, nobody understands that.

– You can never tell.

– I'm easy, Mark said. What are all these empty spaces?

– Shutting up shop.

– That's out of all proportion. I say out. When I say out they
accuse me of dogma.

– They wouldn't dream of it.

– What do you mean, dogma?

– Up you get.

– Up guards.

– Come on.

– Up.

They walked up Oxford Street and across the roads to Grape
Street. Mark clutched the bus stop.

– Who hath seen the mobled queen?

– She caught a tube, Pete said.

Inside the bus Mark lolled asleep. Pete helped him off at the pond. They lunged down the middle of the street.

– Hold hard, Pete said.

– I have savage cause!

– You're elected. Where's your key?

They stumbled into the hall.

– Pete, Mark said, beginnings can't be observed.

Pete pushed the bedroom door open, switched on the light. They fell inside.

– Get 'em off.

– *Oblomov* by Goncharov.

Pete sat on the floor, lifted Mark's leg and pulled off a shoe.

– Ivan Ivanovitch, lurched Mark, has shot himself.

– Do me a favour. Off!

In his shirt, Mark crawled under the sheets. Pete, sitting on the bed, stared at him.

– Pete!

– Yes.

– There's no doubt.

– None at all, Pete said.

Twenty-four

– I've seen a ghost.
– What? Mark turned.
They were sitting in the Swan café in the early evening. Behind the counter the mother and daughter spoke together in Italian, serving icecream through the window.
– Isn't that Len, just about to be run over?
– I don't believe it.
Len made his way between two buses and a furniture van, reached the pavement and peered in through the door.
– We don't want to know you, Mark said.
He walked smiling to the table.
– Merry Christmas.
– I thought you were supposing to be forging new lands, said Pete. What have you done with Paris?
– I left, Len said, sitting down. I've only been back two days.
– Two days? Mark said. What have you been doing?
– Recuperating.
– You look as though the police of twelve continents are after you, Pete said. Why did you leave?
Len looked at them.
– How are things?
– Fine, Mark said. Why did you leave?
– Why did I leave? There's only one reason I left. I don't mind telling you. All right. I'll tell you.
– Well? Pete said.
– It was because of the cheese.
– The cheese?
– The cheese. Stale Camembert cheese. It got me in the end. It all came out, I can tell you, in about twentyeight goes. My temperature was fivehundred of the best, without stretching

141

it. I couldn't stop shivering and I couldn't stop squatting. It got me all right. It always gets you in the end. You know what it's like? Someone hits the ball, you grab at it, and it hits you straight in the eye, or in this case, the belly. I'm all right now. I only go three times a day now. I can more or less regulate it. Once in the morning. A quick dash before lunch. Another quick dash after tea, and then I'm free to do what I want. I don't think you two can understand. The trouble with Camembert, you see, is that it doesn't die. In fact, it only begins to live when you swallow it. This particular Camembert, at least. A German I got to know there used to take it to bed with him. He was the master though, I can tell you that.

- He had it taped, eh? Mark said.
- You're right. He had it taped. He used to treat it brutally, that cheese. He would bite into it, really bite into it, and then concentrate. The sweat used to come out on his nose, but he always won. I never saw him eat anything else, except now and then a tomato and one or two mushrooms. I hate to say it, but his piss stank worse than Old Testament Rabbis.
- You were in Paris for over a week, Pete said. What else happened?
- I can't remember, Len said. It's blotted everything else out. Whenever I think of Paris I just think of cheese.
- Look, Mark said. Come on. What else happened? Why did you leave?

Len shook his head and smiled.

- No, he said. It was that cheese, that's all. It was the cheese.

Twenty-five

She opened the door.

– Ah.

– Isn't it warm?

– Come here, Pete said.

She sat by him on the sofa and he put his head on her lap.

– Somebody stuffed rubbish down the lavatory at work today, he winked. Blocked up the drain. I was under suspicion for a time. But they're wrong. Well off the track. I have other ways to work.

She stroked his forehead.

– You work too hard.

– It's a working world.

He moved his feet on to the sofa arm.

– How are you?

– Fine.

– I popped into the library on the way home, he said. For a solid hour I was looking through books on dogs, horses, anthropology, psychology, poetic works, oilengines, how to be a lifeboatman and the inside story of a werewolf. Have you ever been a werewolf?

– How would I know?

– A vampire bat?

– I suppose you have.

– Me? I'm a cleanliving customer.

Shadows prowled the room.

– Len's back.

– Len? That was quick.

– He's keeping something under his hat. Wouldn't say why, what, anything.

– There's always this secrecy, this funny business, she said.

– Funny business?

– You never know why, what, anything.

– Oh, I don't know.

– It's confusion, she said. I don't believe –

– What?

– I don't believe everyone need live like that.

– There's no need, no.

– No.

– What are you going to buy me for my birthday?

– Oh yes. What do you want?

– I want a book, he said. I want a wellbound book that'll enlighten me. No long words. Big print.

– All right.

– Eh, I was thinking. Do you ever dream about me?

– You know I do.

– You should put a stop to that.

– Should I?

She looked down at his face, turned her head to the window.

– Pete.

– Yes?

– I want to ask you something.

– Mmn?

– I need a rest.

– What?

– I need a rest.

– A rest?

– Yes.

– What do you mean?

– I'm worn out.

He sat up and swung round to face her.

– I need quiet. I need rest.

He stood up.

– Rest?

– Yes.

– What are you talking about?

She sat still.

- Rest from what?
- From –
- From what?
- Us.

Pete scratched the back of his head.

- Why? What's the matter?
- I'm tired.
- Are you?

He walked over to the window and looked out.

- Only for a little while.
- How long?
- Just – about a fortnight.
- It's not all highvoltage, all the time? Is it?
- No.
- Well?
- But I'm tired.
- What do you want to do with your fortnight?
- Nothing.
- I can't see your face.
- Can't you?
- I can't see your face in this light. Look at me.
- I am.
- Can you see me?
- Yes. You're white in the window.
- You're wearing my dress.
- Yes.
- You didn't have to do that.
- What do you mean?

He lit a cigarette and smiled.

- OK, Ginny. I'll chalk it up in the book. Not the black book, the red one.

The match burnt slowly in the pressing dark. He watched it grow to his finger and sharply spun the ashed stick through the open window. Outside, the night was black.

- Anyone would think we're in Eskimoland, he said. Before you can cut up a corpse the night's as black as a beetle.

He turned. She was looking at him.
- OK. You want a rest. Have one. I wish you luck.
- Thank you.
- Two weeks. Don't worry. I won't fly in at your window like a vampire bat. It's not my bloodsucking season.
She walked to him at the window and touched his arm.
- No. Don't kiss me. That I do not want.

III

Twenty-six

– What did you say?
– I never said anything.
– You never said anything. No. But you're at it again.
– At it? said Mark.
– You're at it again.
– It's four o'clock. I'm tired.
– What do you do when you're tired, go to bed?
– That's right.
– You sleep like a log.
– Of course.
– What do you do when you wake up?
– Walk down the day.
– Do you look where you're going?
– I go where I go.
– I want to ask you a question, Len said.
– No doubt.
– Are you prepared to answer questions?
– No.
– But you say you don't ask. If you don't answer and you
  don't ask, what do you do?
– Walk down the day.
– And sleep like a log?
– That's right.
– What do you do in the day when you're not walking?
– Is that the question?
– Eh?
– Is that the question?
– What question?
– Go on.
– What question?

- You were going to ask me a question.
- What about it?
- Is that the question?
- This isn't the question I was going to ask you.
- What is it?
- It's another question.
- It's all another question.
- Well, come on.
- All right. Go on, Mark said.

Len stood up.

- What do you mean, go on? he said. I've asked you a question. You haven't answered it.
- What was it?
- What do you do in the day when you're not walking?
- I rest.
- Where do you find a restingplace?
- Here and there.
- By consent?
- Invariably.
- But you're not particular?
- Yes, I'm particular.
- You choose your restingplace?
- Sometimes.
- And that might be anywhere?
- What do you want?
- Have you a home?
- No.
- What did you say?
- No.
- So where are you?
- Between homes.

Len sat down.

- Do you believe in God?
- What?
- Do you believe in God?
- Who?

- God.
- God?
- Do you, or don't you, believe in God?
- Do I believe in God?
- Yes.
- Would you say that again?
- Have a biscuit.
- Thanks.
- They're your biscuits.
- There's two left. Have one yourself.

Len stood up.

- You don't understand. You'll never understand.
- Really?
- Do you know what the point is? Do you know what it is?
- No, what?
- The point is, who are you? Not why or how, not even what.
  I can see what, perhaps, clearly enough. I can see something perhaps, of what you are. But when all's said and
  done, who are you? It's no use saying you know who you
  are just because you tell me you can fit your particular key
  into a particular slot which will only receive your particular
  key because that's not foolproof and certainly not conclu-
  sive. Just because you're inclined to make these statements
  of faith has nothing to do with me. It's none of my business.

Len walked about the room, his hands stabbing.

- Occasionally, as I say, I believe I perceive a little of what
  you are, but that's pure accident. Pure accident on both our
  parts. The perceived and the perceiver. It must be accident.
  We depend on such accidents to continue, and when we
  accidentally perceive, or appear to do so, it's not important
  then that that might also be hallucination.

He stood in the corner of the room.

- What you are, or appear to be to me, or appear to be to you,
  at any given time, changes so quickly, so horrifyingly, I
  certainly can't keep up with it and I'm damn sure you can't
  either. But who you are, I can't even begin to recognize,

151

and sometimes I recognize it so wholly, so forcibly, I can't look, and how can I be certain of what I see? You have no number. What is there to locate, so as to be certain, to have some surety, to have some rest from this whole bloody racket? You're the sum of so many reflections. How many reflections? Whose reflections? Is that what you consist of? What scum does the tide leave? What happens to the scum? When does it happen? I've seen what happens. But I can't speak when I see it. I can only point a finger. I can't even do that. The scum is broken and sucked back. I don't see where it goes. What have I seen? What have I seen, the scum or the essence? What about it? Does all this give you the right to stand there and tell me you know who you are? It's a bloody impertinence. There's a great desert and there's a wind stopping. Perhaps you can convince me. Can you convince me? But you can hardly do that, ever, because you're always saying you know who you are and therefore I can't trust you. If you could only say something I could believe or begin to believe I could kill you with a clean blade and not think twice about it. But I can never kill you because you can never give me the answer I want. Neither you nor Pete. You'd both better watch out. It's all so simple. You may be Pete's Black Knight. He may be your Black Knight. But I know one thing, and that is I'm cursed with two, two Black Knights, and until I know who you are how can I ever know who I am?

– That's out of order.
– No it isn't.
– What's all this about Black Knights?
– The one there. The Black Knight. Behind the curtains. Pete's yours and you're his. You live off each other.
– We get on like a house on fire.
– I'm glad to hear it.
– All right, Mark said, standing. I've only got one thing to say.
– Be careful.

– I don't know what we want. But whatever it is we won't get
  it.
– Why not?
– Because we've got it.
Len sat down and closed his eyes.

Twenty-seven

– Hullo mate.

– Hullo mate. Come in.

– I thought I'd take a strawzy round to see ya, Mark said.

– Sit down, Pete said. Still raining?

– No. Was it?

– Well, wasn't it?

– No, not for the last threequarters of an hour.

– You've been walking for threequarters of an hour? I didn't think you had it in you.

Mark laughed and began to fill a pipe.

– Where'd you get that?

– Mine. I thought I'd give it an airing.

– What are you smoking?

– Three Nuns.

– It's got a good pong.

– Yes, it makes a change.

– You're gassing me out.

– Yes, it's in good shape, this pipe. I've just given it a good clean out.

– Want a drink?

– Don't bother.

– Cleaning pipes, stretching your legs. Where'd you get all this energy?

– You know that girl, Sonia?

– Who?

– She was with me at that party.

– Oh yes.

– I'm seeing her tonight.

– What's that got to do with it?

– Well, I've decided a pipe'd be up her street.

- Why?
- Well, Mark said, it emphasizes the old polarity.
- Up your polarity.
- You've got to be able to cater, you know.
- Who for, women?
- No. I agree. There's no necessity. It's all a lark.
- Mind if I smoke? Pete said, lighting a cigarette.

A spurt of rain hit the window.

- There it is, Pete said.
- Look at it.
- Yes.
- It'll be a quick autumn this year, Mark said. Take my tip.
- I think you're right.

They watched the rain.

- I'm worn out, Mark said, with the heat. That's just the job.
- Yes.

Mark poked at the funnel of his pipe.

- Well, how are you? he said.
- Not so bad.
- What have you been up to?

Pete shivered and put on his jacket.

- You're not looking so good, Mark said.
- As a matter of fact, things are a little topsywhatsaname at
  the moment.
- .How?
- Aah, Pete grimaced, it's a stupid business.
- What's happened?
- Have you seen Virginia at all?
- Virginia? No.
- Well, I haven't either.
- Oh?
- She's done the dirty on me. It's finished.
- What's all this?
- She's gone down the drain, Pete said. It's not worth the
  candle. She's changed her spots.
- What's been going on?

– Aah! Pete said. She's been mixing with some crowd in Soho, that's all. She's gone gay. It's all up.

– I thought I hadn't seen her about.

– Yes, we agreed she should have a rest. For a fortnight. But she didn't come back, that's all.

– Well.

– No, Pete said. If that's the way she wants it she can have it.

– You agreed she should have a rest?

– Yes. All right. Don't think I didn't see her point. I did.

– She needed it.

– Look here, Mark. She needed a rest and she got it. I've admitted it. But considering the burden we've both had to carry all this time we'd managed more than well, in my opinion. But all right, I agreed she should have a rest. What does she do? Chucks it all out of the window. For what? I tell you, she's a lost cause as far as I'm concerned. You know the kind of people she's running about with, the places she sits in? I won't even bother to describe them.

– But she's not your territory, Mark said. How can you sanction her actions?

– I'm not, old boy, Pete said. I'm passing my last comment on this situation.

– Yes, I can see your point.

– I've driven her to drink. All right. Let's turn over the page.

The rain slid on the pane.

– I've had enough.

– Should I go and see her? Mark said.

– What for?

– Find out what she's up to.

– I've told you what she's up to.

– Yes, but it may not be as simple as that.

– What do you mean?

– Maybe I can do some good.

– Good?

– Find out how things really stand.

Pete stood up and shut the top half of the window. He

returned to the table and sat down.

– There's nothing to do, he said, nothing worth doing.

– I don't know.

– Yes, it's been a kick in the guts. I admit it. But I'll tell you straight – I don't want any more of it.

– I'll get in touch with her. See how things stand, Mark said.

– In what capacity?

– As your friend.

– That's your business, if you want to see her. I'm bankrupt. It'll all be over and done with soon. All I need is a breath of fresh air.

They sat in the room.

– Still raining.

– I think it's in for the night, Pete said.

Twenty-eight

- Virginia?
- Hello?
- Mark.
- Hello.
- I got your card.
- Good.
- I was going to phone you anyway.
- Were you?
- What are you doing?
- Nothing.
- I'm at home.
- I'll come round.
- Now?
- Yes.
- Right. See you.

- Well, what's all this? Mark smiled, as they sat down.
The room was quiet. She crossed her legs.
- All what?
- Pete.
- There's nothing to it, she said. It's finished.
- Just like that?
- There's nothing else to say.
- Nothing?
- No.
She opened her bag and took out a packet of cigarettes. Mark
stood up and, bending over her chair, struck a match. She sat
back in the armchair. He sat down.
- So there's nothing else to say, eh?
- It couldn't go on any longer. Have you got an ashtray?

– Put it in the grate.

She flicked ash into the grate and smoothed her hair over her ear.

– Tch, tch, she smiled. Do you keep this place in order?

– Not me. A charlady.

– What about the washing up?

– I do that.

– Have you done it today?

– Today? No.

– Shall I do it?

– No.

She stretched her legs on the carpet and blew smoke.

– I've washed up in your kitchen before.

– I know.

He coughed and banged his chest.

– Bad, she said.

– Well look here. You're not going back to Pete?

– No. Do you take anything for that cough?

– No.

He cleared his throat.

– I hear you've been gadding about.

– You could call it that.

– You could, eh?

– I've been going about with a man called Tucker.

– From the West Country?

– He's a Red Indian.

– So am I.

– No you're not.

– What am I?

She flicked ash into the grate.

– Tucker, eh?

– Tucker. There's nothing else to say.

– Well, there must be something to say about something, Mark said.

– I suppose so.

– Give me your fag. You'll burn your fingers.

He took it from her hand, stubbed it out and sat down again.

- How's school?
- We're on holiday, she said.
- Oh yes, of course.
- So are you.
- Yes, you're right.
- A long one.
- Quite long, he said.
- When are you going to do some work?
- I'll have to soon.
- Where?
- Anywhere.

She opened her bag.

- Have another one.
- No. Have one of mine.

Bending over her, he lit her cigarette.

- Thanks.
- That's a lovely dress, he said, sitting down.
- Thank you.
- Not at all.

Mark looked at her across the room.

- Why are you looking at me?
- The same reason I always looked at you.
- You're making me blush.
- Why did you send me that card?
- I wanted to see you.
- Why?
- Why did you phone me?
- I told Pete I'd phone you.
- Oh?
- I wanted to speak to you. It's a long time since we spoke to each other.
- We've hardly ever spoken to each other, Virginia said.

He stood up and stubbed his cigarette.

- Give me yours, he said, I'll put it out.

He took it from her hand and stubbed it out. He sat down.

– Tell me.
– Yes? said Virginia.
– Can you run through snow leaving no footprint?
– I think so.
– You must be able to do that, you know.
– I think I could.
– Are you sure?
– Don't you think I could?
– Yes, I do.
– You knew it all the time.
– I've always known it, he said. It's there, in your eyes.
– Was it always there?
– Always. And in your body.
– Was it always in my body?
– Yes, always.
– And in your body too, she said.
– Really?
– Yes.
– Your body, he said. It's always been in all of your body.
– Always.
– I've never seen your legs above your knees.
– No.
– Lift your skirt up.
– Mmn?
– Lift your skirt up.
– Like this?
– Yes. Go on.
– Like this?
– Leave it.
– Like this?
– Uncross your legs.
– Like this?

– So he thinks I'm a fool?
They lay on the bed.
– He thinks that of everyone.

161

– But he has said to you that I am a fool?

– He's said so many things.

– No, but I want to know exactly.

– Why?

– Tell me.

– I've told you.

– You've heard him say it?

– From all he's ever said to me about you, she said, I don't think he respects you.

– He doesn't respect me and he thinks I'm a fool.

– But can't you see, she said, he doesn't respect anyone. He hates everyone.

– All these years, eh?

– Let's forget him.

Mark sat on the edge of the bed and scratched his head.

– What I can't understand is, if he thinks I'm a fool, why bother to see me?

– He uses you, and everyone, she said, touching his back. Forget him.

– What sort of game has he been playing?

– Look, it's all right, she said. What the hell?

– What do you mean?

– He hasn't harmed me. I've survived.

– Yes – you're all right, but there's another thing.

– Look at me. Come and lie down.

Mark looked at her.

– Why are you worrying so much about him?

– You don't understand, he said.

– He doesn't worry me any more.

– Do you mean to say, do you mean that after all this time with him, the cord just snaps, snap, just like that?

– It was frayed.

She drew him down to her.

– Do you know what I'd like now?

– What?

– I'd like him to walk in and see us, she said. Naked. In each

162

other's arms.
- Would you?

She clasped him.

- Look, she whispered, you might as well make the most of me, because we'll only last about a week.
- What are you talking about? Mark said. You and me?
- Kiss me.

Mark kissed her and sat up.

- I'll tell you one thing, he said. He's made a grave error. I'm not a fool.

Twenty-nine

– Hello Mark.

– Hello.

– What are you doing?

– Nothing.

– Going to invite me in?

– Sure.

They walked down the stairs.

– Well, Pete said, what are you doing with yourself?

– When's that?

– Now.

– Nothing.

– You look as if you're up to something.

– Don't believe it.

Mark sat down at the table.

– Len's in hospital, Pete said.

– Len?

– Yes.

– What's the matter with him?

– His bowels wouldn't work. He came a cropper.

– When was this?

– A few days ago, Pete said, sitting down. It's not serious.

– Hmmn.

Mark looked out of the window at the sky.

– You got a weatherglass in this house? Pete said.

– No.

– They're very handy.

– Why?

– You can see how the world stands. It's colder today.

– You know there's no weatherglass here.

– I knew a bloke once who always carried one with him.

Pocket size. His own invention.

Mark brought a nailfile from his pocket and probed his right ear.

– Well, Pete said, what have you been doing with yourself?

– When?

– Since I saw you.

– This and that.

– This and what?

– That.

– It sticks out a mile.

Mark wiped the file on his thigh.

– What about writing? Done any writing lately?

– No.

– Lost the knack?

– I wouldn't say that.

– Good, Pete said.

Mark filed his thumbnail.

– Do you want to bowl along and see Len?

– When, now?

– Yes, Pete said. Are you busy?

– No.

– Right.

– All right.

– It's visiting time.

Mark probed his left ear and flicked wax from the file.

– What's up?

Mark put the file in his pocket.

– What? he said.

– What's up with you?

– What do you mean?

– You're wearing a gasmask.

– Not me.

Pete, smiling, stood up.

– Are you ready?

– Yes.

They left the house. The day was dull. They passed the pond and walked towards the hospital.

– It's a fine old day, Pete said. A bit chilly.

They walked on.

– The leaves are breaking up. That's not a bad phrase. What do you think?

– What about?

They crossed the road by the Electricity Company and walked on.

– Old Len got them to phone me at work. Just in time. I gave in my notice yesterday.

– Did you?

They passed the back of the cemetery.

– Eh, how's your capital? When are you going to do a bit more acting?

– Haven't thought about it.

They walked by a waste of bombed ground.

– Ah well, Pete said.

A brisk wind rattled the leaves and paperbags. They passed the firestation and approached the hospital.

– Read any good books lately? Pete asked.

– No.

They turned in at the hospital gates.

– Mr Weinstein? Pete said.

– Ward C.

They walked through the building, up the stairs to the first floor, and into the ward. Visitors sat by the beds. A number of patients wore earphones. The nurses collected at the far end, by a tray of flowers. Pete and Mark walked up the ward.

– Don't think he'd be behind a screen. Do you? Pete said.

– No hawking or canvassing.

They turned.

– Didn't see you, said Pete.

– It's not surprising, said Len, lowering the sheet.

They sat on each side of his bed.

– You got here.

– We got here, Mark said.

– Well, what's all this? said Pete.

166

- I'm as right as rain, Len said, now. They can't do enough for me.
- Why?
- Because I'm no trouble. These nurses, they treat me like a king.

The nurses stood talking by the tray of flowers.

- Like a king, Len said.
- Have a fag, said Pete, handing one to Mark.
- It suits me down to the ground, said Len.
- Staying long? Pete asked.
- I'm out in two days. I'm in running order.

Mark turned to look at the nurses.

- They're a very good lot, Len muttered.

Mark turned back. Smoke slid from his nostrils.

- You look as though you've caught a crab, Len said.
- What?
- You looked undernourished.
- Do I?
- Pleasant ward, Pete said.
- It's ideal.

Mark and Pete looked about the ward.

- Best quality blankets, home cooking, Len said, the lot.

Mark looked up at the ceiling.

- Not too low, not too high, Len said, and broke into a fit of coughing. Where's the gobbing tin?

Mark looked under the bed. Pete lifted the chamberpot and held it up. Len spat into the urine.

- You're pissing well, Mark said.
- I thought you'd say that.
- I thought you were at death's door, when they phoned, Pete said. I was going to Petticoat Lane to buy you a secondhand crucifix.
- I told them you were my next of kin.

Pete blew a smokering.

- By the way, Mark, he said, what's happened to your pipe?
- Nothing's happened to it.

– Did it work?

– You smoking a pipe? Len asked.

– No.

– Well, Pete said, I chucked my hand in yesterday.

– How? Len said.

– I gave in my notice.

– Why?

– Enough's enough.

– What are you going to do?

– I'm after something.

– Let's open a business.

– Well, Len, said Mark, you're looking very well.

The ward shone. Through the bright window leaves breaking. Mark dropped his cigarette on the floor and ground it out.

– You'll have me prosecuted, Len said.

By the tray of flowers the nurses talked.

– What's it like out? Len said.

– Bit chilly, said Pete, today.

– Bound to be.

– The sun's come out.

– That means rain.

– Does it?

– Well, Mark, said Len, bring off the treble chance this week?

– Not me.

The visitors were moving from the beds. The nurses, dispersing, walked down the ward.

– Who's driving the tank?

– What? said Pete.

– Who's driving the tank?

– Don't ask me. We've been walking up the road back to back.

– You've what?

Len looked at Mark.

– You've been walking up the road back to back?

Pete stubbed his cigarette in a saucer on the bedside table. The nurses moved along the ward.

– You're not supposed to sit on the bed, Len said. You're
supposed to sit on the chair.
– Well, Pete said, we'll leave you to it. Knock us up when you
get out.
– Yes, Mark said, knock us up.
– How do I know if you'll be in?

Pete and Mark left the hospital and walked towards the pond.
The sun was gone and a light rain slipped.
– Horizontal personalities, those places, Pete said. You're the
only vertical. Makes you feel dizzy.
Mark turned his collar up. They passed the firestation.
– You ever been inside one of those places? Pete asked.
– I'm not sure. I can't remember.
– Right, Pete said. Bollocks.
He turned his collar up. They passed the bombed site.
– All right, Mark said, scowling in the rain.
They walked on over the broken leaves.
– Why do you knock on my door?
– What?
– Come on. Why do you knock on my door?
– What are you talking about?
They passed the back of the cemetery.
– It's a straight question.
– I call to see you, mate.
– Why?
– Tired of my own company.
– But what do you want with me? Why come and see me?
– Why?
– Either you know what you're doing or you don't know
what you're doing. Either way I don't like the smell.
– Take it easy Mark.
– But I think you know bloodywell what you're doing. I think
you've been playing a double game for years, as far as I'm
concerned, as far as everybody's concerned.
– Don't push me, mate.

They crossed the road by the Electricity Company and continued towards the pond.

- You've been using me as you use every bugger. In actual fact you don't give a fuck for any of us.
- You've started something you might regret, Pete said. But all right. Go on. Get down to brass tacks.

In heavier rain they approached the pond, the water spitting and breaking about the islands.

- You're twofaced, Mark said. You've treated me as one thing to my face and behind my back it's been quite a different matter.
- Behind your back? This is infantile. Who's been pouring the poison?

They stopped at the corner of the pond.

- You've been stringing me along, Mark said. You've been giving me the grapes for years.
- Someone's been doing a bit of graft here, Pete said. You're dropping a big clangor. But who's told you what? Look, it's wet. Come and have a drink.

They walked across the road and into a pub. Mark sat down. Pete went to the counter and returned with two beers.

- Drink up. I think you've got one or two things somewhat alltoballsed, he said.
- Your behaviour to Virginia, Mark said, leaning across the table, has been criminal for years.
- Watch yourself, Pete said. You're out of your depth already.
- It's been criminal from all angles. And I'll tell you another thing, Mark said, for nothing. I slept with her last night.

The room stopped. Then Pete heard the chink in the echo of glass. Now standing, he looked down at Mark.

- It's finished, he spat, and left the pub.

Thirty

Returning, after he had finished his drink, to his flat, Mark walked down the stairs in the dark, and in the dark passed through the living room. He stood at the kitchen window looking out at his garden. Becoming dark in the rain the garden shivered. The rain, clouting sideways over the shrubs, turned the leaves dark. There was no sky. He watched a cat crawl through the fence and leap the lawn to the lilacarch, through which it passed. He stared after it. It did not return, nor by any movement disclose itself, if it was still in the garden. As the traps of dark shut about him he remained heavy in the silent room. As the night locked, he looked out upon it, through the window. In the fall of night, as swift as it was complete, the rain fell black, and the foliage became part of a mass, and the garden an anonymous receding, and he found at length only his dim reflection in the glass, to look at, in the forefront of the darkness, brought by a faint lamplight from beyond the front door, moving diminishing through the length of the flat, through all the doors left open. The fall of the rain now put forward its hiss, consuming the silence, and as it maintained a constant motion, shuddering the darkness which in turn blacked it out, as the walls made their sound, as the ceiling distended, as the room stood aloud, mammoth and shapeless, as night had been made, he sat down imprisoned facing the stairs.

Later, the remains of the rain slapping on the windowsill, he looked up and saw Pete in the hallway, still.

– Are you there? Pete said.

– Yes.

Pete came down the stairs into the room and sat down.

– I want you to listen, he said.

He sat upright.

171

– It won't take long.

Mark turned to the wall.

– You don't surprise me, Pete said. But we'll leave that. I can speak. There's something to be said. Not that you've surprised me.

Because you haven't. But that's another thing. A couple of hours, you see, make all the difference. There's this to be done with. It's time. I'll say it. It's best. You can say what you like, if you like, afterwards. Fair enough?

You see, I want to understand. What I can't sympathize with, I can only try to condone, by way of friendship. But quite frankly you must be mad to sweep it all away in a gust of new affection.

I like the way you've painted me black. It's blunt, but erroneous. I can afford a joke, but this one has gone too far.

It was a kick in the balls, I admit it. Shows I'm still subject to human pains. That's all. Illuminating in a way, but nothing more. The bones. The bones are far more interesting than the soft parts of the belly.

No. My motives were never inspired by any great love or respect for Virginia. They were neither unselfish or generous. So you can be all the things I can't be to her. All right. Why not? I considered her a great asset to me when we had something in common, but it was very little and quite honestly very seldom.

I can bury all that without too much of a strain.

Listen. I've liked you when you were positive, generous and friendly. When you revealed yourself. All I can do at the moment is appreciate it.

It was a bullet. But there's nothing in my hair about Virginia. What you two get up to is your own business.

But the point is this. You don't care about me because in a fairish way you've fallen short of the truth. Well short. What have you got against me? Lies? Did I talk behind your back? Is that the sum total of my virtue? The whole business is ludicrous. Of course I've spoken behind your back. Of your qualities and your faults. If you complain of one will you do without the other? Perhaps so. But you'll do quite well without my praise.

I'd rather you hit me in the eye than this lark go on. I may go to hell but not for this business. Of course the whole caboodle might well be an efficient idea.

I'll add when I haven't liked you. I haven't liked you when I felt, which I did nearly all the time when we were alone, that I was a bloke you were speaking to between one bed and another. You may find that injurious to the truth. You may feel a lot happened which was worthwhile, which was of value.

If you know me at all, you must know that my personal relationships have nearly always been of secondary importance. My natural disposition is to be alone and play the old joanna. There's always some tune or other. You understand. It's not surprising, you see, that my friends have, however wellmeaning, drained my blood dry.

No, I'm not cutting capers. Perhaps I've got one knacker missing, after all.

What it means, for us, is that I didn't give back what I owed you, because I didn't have the wherewithal to pay. I take it you're mortally sick of bunging your affection down a cesspool. That being in my society was an infection. Or that I've bit the hand that willingly tried to feed me. Or that I've desecrated the temple. But how much of it is true? I haven't got failings I can't admit in the face of a true reproach, but how much of what is true, and who is alive to reproach me?

Can you put a word to it? Because I know all about it, better than you. Believe me. Voluble and unclean and all the rest of it. I did a ridiculous thing sometime ago, which I doubt if you'll understand. I sold my better soul to God and he has paid me dividends.

I can survive to write out the new Psalms of David. Perhaps you are unaware that he is one of my ideal men. I have believed in Christ but that was purely voluntary. But as for the terrors, there's no word for them yet. They're something quite different. Lunatics believe in them and regard them as relevant and decisive. It's a moot point.

But I believe there's more to you and me than this abortion we called friendship. We misunderstood it and each other, and practically everything else. _

You must have lost your true self if you can't listen to what I'm saying and get something from it.

What I want you to get, above all, is that we ought to have the opportunity to blacken each other's eye, if we decide it's necessary. Also, that people like you and me, who aren't an unmixed blessing, ought to survive a love affair without being vicious, stupid or blinded.

That's it.

Mark remained still.

I suppose you've got something to say.

– Yes. Mark said, I have.
He turned from the wall and sat up.
– Yes, I think so.
He looked into the grate and across the room.
– The point is, you see –
He stretched and looked up at the ceiling.
– My trouble is, he said, that I have to convince myself that
you don't really consider me a cunt. At least I have to
assume you don't, before I can say anything at all.

So I'll assume that you don't, for the moment.

I've listened.

You see, I can appreciate, Pete, that you reserve the right to
bestow contempt. So do I. I can also appreciate that a great
deal of your time is spent trying to reconcile it with something else, which you consider as valuable.

But it seems to me that when it comes down to it, you
inhabit a stronghold of contempt from which you can't
escape. You can reconcile in theory. You may believe it
possible. But in fact everything is, and must be for you,
cooked in your oven.

You can't cook in anyone else's oven.

You say friendships and whatnot have never been productive. Most of the time then, I was under a delusion. In truth
you've never shared. You've been incapable. So I've been
up the garden. I resent it. I thought there might have been
at times a sharing, a meeting. I was wrong. And you knew
it, always.

175

The point is, to what extent are you, in fact, responsible? Are you to be treated as responsible and concerned or not? I mean, what does concern you? Surely not your friends as they wish to be, but only in so far as they can fit your requirements. Where they fail to do so, contempt, by your own logic, is the only outcome. It's their epitaph. They become for you an academic exercise in failure. Not because they themselves have necessarily failed, but simply that in attempting to retain what is their own, they have failed you.

You have no other criterion.

You've always known I was a lost cause, yet you've continued to knock on my door. Why? Because you considered me your equal? Not by a long chalk. It was because you didn't really take me seriously. In your terms I was damned from the kickoff, beyond redemption. You couldn't work your salvation on me as you might have done on Len and Virginia, so because I was outside your moral consideration association was permissible. You could use me as a shining example of the wrong way. As copy.

But I can see. There is another thing I can see. Don't think I can't. We have met. You and me. One time at a bus-stop, we were drunk. But then when you were alone? I can't trust you when you're alone.

It's what you are alone that you must be in me. Or nothing. What's the point, any longer, of playing a game? I can't see any profit.

You talk of bones. What are the bones? That you've been a bloodsucker, and I think you'd do well to admit it.

We, the lot of us, have only been necessary to perform a

caper in your pageant, to pay homage at your court. Listen. The function of a friend, that you would call a friend, must be that of an ambassador to yourself from yourself. A go-between. Then he's a man of your soul. But enough's enough.

We've all been your accomplices but mine is the grossest fault. I've let you get away with it for too long.

The point is, I've admired. I've admired you on the war-path. I've stayed in the hunt because I've enjoyed killing with you, however many rats I may have smelt. Because that's the sort of bloke, the sort of jackal I can be too. I smile, I think that's a good smile, I look in the mirror to see what it's like. So you never really got me on your kitchen staff. I played you at the same time. It's all been a dirty doublecross. Sure I've used you.

But at the same time I know what's been good. I know what's been real, in despite of us both. I know what has stood, what part of the cheese won't go bad. Because cohabitation brings forth, even in a monster with two heads, something sound in the body of the creature.

I lay the thing bare, but that can't alter the fact that you have always had an irrevocable lodging in my house, and I don't regret it. It remains so. But too often you've brought your own sheets, your own blankets, everything. You had to kip on your own terms. But you couldn't change the furniture inside because I had my feet fixed. I know where I live. You're not a fool. You knew I was as cunning. But with Virginia nothing could stop you. You may have lost a king-dom but it was your own destruction did it. You buggered the issue. I was needed. Do you know that? But I took nothing from you. It was all your own work.

You may have lost but I haven't won. That's what you want to get into your nut.

She needed a change of air. You exist, but just remember that so does she, in her own right. And I too, exist.

All right. I'm willing to meet you for a cup of tea. But I won't be your Fool and I won't be your Black Knight.

He stopped, sat back, waited.

  – Well, Pete said.
His eyes screwed, he rubbed his mouth.
  – Well, well, he said, that's very interesting.

If we are going to define what we are, and our territorial limitations, then I'm afraid I can't honestly do it for myself. Being simpler and saner you may find the job within your scope.

I can't say though how pleased I am that you do recognize my faults. I must believe that what you point out is a working deficiency, quite of some magnitude, but it's one inevitable to the kind of way I have declared for myself.

I've always known that neither you nor Virginia were the gods of my inner sanctum. I had and have weighed you both as carefully and as honestly as I can. And I find that even in ordinary decencies you have been ignorant and unworthy, not even when I pushed you to it.

Experience is the testing ground. This one has shown I can survive and not shove the dead on other people. It has left both of you alive. See to it then. Buck your ideas up, because there's an allpervading stink.

What you seem to say is that I let you down. Both of you prefer to blame me. I haven't tried to make this a cause fatale, but if both of you don't watch out it might very well become fatal, for both of you. It'll be your death and your suffocation. Pass the word on. You can do her, and yourself, a much bigger favour than you've managed up till now.

Where does it all come from? Yes, I admit, to a great and overwhelming extent it comes from me. The whole thing is a child of my womb. I can apologize to you, but you alone could not forgive me. It is not in your power. This is what you must listen to. I cannot, it is sinful, to apologize for your faults.

You made of your friendship a tool to bludgeon me with and you went off and slept with Virginia. I feel very angry about this, not without cause. I would have avoided the subject because I was prepared to have you as a friend. I don't believe - in fact I shan't - hold rancour against you for it. If anything I can like you more. But let there be no doubt at all about where we stand. For this, by itself and alone, to me the virtue. Let me bring it into the open.

Up to this point and no more, I have been proved a wiser and a better person than any of you. I am, I think it, though you may not believe it, a god in my essential dimensions. Of course, I cannot be worshipped. I have to be lived with. But I am sick, nearly to death and to suicide, of this supposition by Len, by Virginia, and by you most of all, that I have anything at all to do with this cycle of love and despair that is essentially your motive and business. I haven't. I can help you. I can pray for you. A prophet in his own country. But it's ridiculous to think I can live with you.

You have all tried to be friends with me, and therefore for as long and as well as I can I shall be grateful for it. But if you get inside and eat my stomach I will always bite back - in spades.

179

I have been the longsufferer. You have done the jumping up and down on my belly, you have tried to bash my head in, have tried to infect my bloodstream, have tried to cut up my bowels for mincemeat. You have done the deserting, have been small and smaller, parasitic, strangers when I needed you. You have observed, never really been sympathetic. My firework exhibitions have amused you. I have laid myself on tap. There has been no reward but that which I expected. A lot of desecrating, bloodsucking talkers and natterers over cups of tea and the certainty of perishing by vanity, ignorance and moral suicide.

I will say that about some things you have been more or less on the mark.

If I am a god at all it is the god of futility and remorse. I have never done anything for you. I should like to. I will try. I'm awake. I'm wide awake.

You can take this or leave it. I think it, however, worthwhile to point out that a granary, if it has no wheat to crush, is bound to be destructive. I haven't been hoodwinked about that. I will yet move worlds when I find my lever. Count yourself lucky, but keep a sense of proportion.

Of course all I have to do to destroy you is to leave you as you wish to be. I could lay a curse on you that would certainly find you out. But I have no wish to avenge myself. I have no need to curse you. There is no end to the objections of good sense. But insofar as the truth is mine so also is its power. That has always been so. So I can give you a tip. What you've got to do is move. While you've got the chance. You're a stagnant pool. You have, quite frankly, the air of a man who is finished.

Your social faults don't interest me, if I could trust you. But you ask too much when you want me to take them as credible. Your morality, your bedmanners, are something I no longer want to interfere in. It's your stink. Carry it. But it's your integrity that's in question and you haven't proved that you're worth it. I am asking you to be honest. It was fear and anger led you to bed. A mess of it. It's true that my integrity has vanished on many occasions. It was frustration and hate that did it. I had at all costs to survive, and I have bitten, cut and slashed with a good will and enjoyed doing it. It was a question of overriding justice. Did I, above everything, believe that my being killed might be not only an overwhelming disaster for me, but an irreplaceable lack in the sum total of human knowledge, and an irreparably lost opportunity for creating good? There is very little on my conscience about that. It's all supposition.

I think you've made a fool of yourself over this bed business. It was a clangor. When the echoes of it die I hope you'll be there to smile at the ruins. You won't by thinking I am wrong. The damn thing will bounce up and give you such a crack in the bollocks you won't know where it comes from.

But if this is the status quo of creation I'll take no more bites out of anybody. The flesh is sour. I'll go hungry. I've had many a laugh at the crumbs Len threw away. I've been alive to the comfort you've both tried to give. Let it be said, even if it damns me, that I appreciate it. But don't let it blind us to the issue. You reproach me because I should be perfect. No. And I can't be dallied out of my spot. Don't entice me with just affection. I have more to offer of that than a dozen of you. Merely listen to the truth. It's shaming to all of us but it may do some good.

You can see the fix I'm in. I'm ready to listen. I will listen intelligently. I will go and understand. Make a journey for it.

But I will not cut my suit entirely to measure you, on a pretext. In a spirit of trying most things are possible. For that reason you can go to hell. We'll both toe the line. I'll come as far as I can. If we can't meet, tough luck. But so far as the truth is concerned, you have a lot farther to travel. If you don't think it worth it, I'm sorry. It would be many miles of good road wasted.

In the past, I haven't been able, or made it my habit, to speak the dog's honest truth about me. This time I have. You have heard it.

Mark did not answer. After a few moments Pete stood up and walked to the window.

 – You've got me, he said, acid and all. On the supposition that it had to be said I've said it.

Mark coughed and spat into the fireplace.

 – I hope the acid hasn't blinded you to the meat and salt.

 – I think, Mark said, it has.

He struck a match and watched it burn.

 – Right, Pete said. I'll let myself out.

Thirty-one

They've stopped eating. It'll be a quick getout when the whistle blows. All their belongings are stacked in piles. But I've heard nothing. What is the cause for alarm? Why is everything packed? Why are they ready for the off?

But they say nothing. They've cut me off without a penny.

And now they've settled down to a wide-eyed kip, crosslegged by the fire. It's insupportable. I'm left in the lurch. Not even a stale frankfurter, a slice of bacon rind, a leaf of cabbage, not even a mouldy piece of salami, like they used to sling me in the days when we told old tales by suntime. They sit, chockfull. But I smell a rat. They seem to be anticipating a rarer dish, a choicer spread.

And this change. All about me the change. The yard as I know it is littered with scraps of catsmeat, pigbollocks, tincans, birdbrains, spare parts of all the little animals, a squelching squealing carpet, all the dwarfs' leavings spittled in the muck, worms stuck in the poisoned shitheaps, the alleys a whirlpool of piss, slime, blood and fruitjuice.

Now all is bare. All is clean. All is scrubbed. There is a lawn. There is a shrub. There is a flower.

1952–1956   Revised 1989